Jean Ingelow

Poems of the Old Days and the New

Jean Ingelow

Poems of the Old Days and the New

ISBN/EAN: 9783337206611

Printed in Europe, USA, Canada, Australia, Japan

Cover: Foto ©Andreas Hilbeck / pixelio.de

More available books at **www.hansebooks.com**

POEMS

OF

THE OLD DAYS

AND

THE NEW.

By JEAN INGELOW.

BOSTON:
ROBERTS BROTHERS.
1885.

TO JEAN INGELOW.

WHEN youth was high, and life was new,
 And days sped musical and fleet,
She stood amid the morning dew,
And sang her earliest measures sweet, —
Sang as the lark sings, speeding fair
To touch and taste the purer air,
To gain a nearer view of Heaven;
'Twas then she sang " The Songs of Seven."

Now, farther on in womanhood,
With trainèd voice and ripened art,
She gently stands where once she stood,
And sings from out her deeper heart.
Sing on, dear Singer! sing again;
And we will listen to the strain,
Till soaring earth greets bending Heaven,
And seven-fold songs grow seventy-seven.

     SUSAN COOLIDGE.

CONTENTS.

POEMS.

———◆———

ROSAMUND.

He blew with His winds, and they were scattered.

'ONE soweth and another reapeth.'
                                          Ay,
Too true, too true.   One soweth — unaware
Cometh a reaper stealthily while he dreams,
Bindeth the golden sheaf, and in his bosom
As 't were between the dewfall and the dawn
Bears it away.   Who other was to blame?
Is it I?   Is it I? — No verily, not I,
'T was a good action, and I smart therefore;
Oblivion of a righteous enmity
Wrought me this wrong.   I pay with my self-ruth
That I had ruth toward mine enemy;
It needed not to slay mine enemy,
Only to let him lie and succourless
Drift to the foot o' the Everlasting Throne;
Being mine enemy. he had not accused
One of my nation there of unkind deeds

1

Or ought the way of war forbids.

Let be!
I will not think upon it.   Yet she was —
O, she was dear; my dutiful, dear child.
One soweth — Nay, but I will tell this out,
The first fyte was the best, I call it such
For now as some old song men think on it.

I dwell where England narrows running north;
And while our hay was cut came rumours up
Humming and swarming round our heads like bees:

' Drake from the bay of Cadiz hath come home,
And they are forth, the Spaniards with a force
Invincible.'

'The Prince of Parma, couched
At Dunkirk, e'en by torchlight makes to toil
His shipwright thousands — thousands in the ports
Of Flanders and Brabant.   An hundred hendes
Transports to his great squadron adding, all
For our confusion.'

' England's great ally
Henry of France, by insurrection fallen,
Of him the said Prince Parma mocking cries,
He shall not help the Queen of England now
Not even with his tears, more needing them
To weep his own misfortune.'

Was that all

The truth? Not half, and yet it was enough
(Albeit not half that half was well believed),
For all the land stirred in the half belief
As dreamers stir about to wake ; and now
Comes the Queen's message, all her lieges bid
To rise, 'lieftenants, and the better sort
Of gentlemen' whereby the Queen's grace meant,
As it may seem the sort that willed to rise
And arm, and come to aid her.
　　　　　　　　　　Distance wrought
Safety for us, my neighbours and near friends,
The peril lay along our channel coast
And marked the city, undefended fair
Rich London. O to think of Spanish mail
Ringing — of riotous conquerors in her street,
Chasing and frighting (would there were no more
To think on) her fair wives and her fair maids.
— But hope is fain to deem them forth of her.

Then Spain to the sacking; then they tear away
Arras and carvèd work. O then they break
And toss, and mar her quaint orfèverie
Priceless — then split the wine kegs, spill the mead,
Trail out the pride of ages in the dust ;
Turn over with pikes her silken merchandise,
Strip off the pictures of her kings, and spoil
Their palaces that nigh five hundred years
Have rued no alien footsteps on the floor,

And work — for the days of miracle are gone —
All unimaginable waste and woe.

Some cried, ' But England hath the better cause ;
We think not those good days indeed are done ;
We look to Heaven for aid on England's side.'
Then other, ' Nay, the harvest is above,
God comforts there His own, and ill men leaves
To run long scores up in this present world,
And pay in another.
             Look not here for aid.
Latimer, poor old saint, died in the street
With nigh, men say, three hundred of his kind,
All bid to look for worse death after death,
Succourless, comfortless, unfriended, curst.
Mary, and Gardiner, and the Pope's man Pole
Died upon down, lulled in a silken shade,
Soothed with assurance of a waiting heaven,
And Peter peering through the golden gate,
With his gold key in 's hand to let them in.'

' Nay, leave,' quoth I, ' the martyrs to their heaven,
And all who live the better that they died.
But look you now, a nation hath no heaven,
A nation's life and work and wickedness
And punishment — or otherwise, I say
A nation's life and goodness and reward
Are here. And in my nation's righteous cause

I look for aid, and cry, So help me God
As I will help my righteous nation now
With all the best I have, and know, and am,
I trust Thou wilt not let her light be quenched;
I go to aid, and if I fall — I fall,
And, God of nations, leave my soul to Thee.'

Many did say like words, and all would give
Of gold, of weapons, and of horses that
They had to hand or on the spur o' the time
Could gather. My fair dame did sell her rings,
So others. And they sent us well equipped
Who minded to be in the coming fray
Whether by land or sea ; my hope the last,
For I of old therewith was conversant.

Then as we rode down southward all the land
Was at her harvesting. The oats were cut
Ere we were three days down, and then the wheat,
And the wide country spite of loathèd threat
Was busy. There was news to hearten us :
The Hollanders were coming roundly in
With sixty ships of war, all fierce, and full
Of spleen, for not alone our sake but theirs
Willing to brave encounter where they might.

So after five days we did sight the Sound,
And look on Plymouth harbour from the hill.

Then I full glad drew bridle, lighted straight,
Ran down and mingled with a waiting crowd.

Many stood gazing on the level deep
That scarce did tremble; 't was in hue as sloes
That hang till winter on a leafless bough,
So black bulged down upon it a great cloud
And probed it through and through with forkèd stabs
Incessant, and rolled on it thunder bursts
Till the dark water lowered as one afraid.

That was afar. The land and nearer sea
Lay sweltering in hot sunshine. The brown beach
Scarce whispered, for a soft incoming tide
Was gentle with it. Green the water lapped
And sparkled at all edges. The night-heavens
Are not more thickly speckled o'er with stars
Than that fair harbour with its fishing craft.
And crowds of galleys shooting to and fro
Did feed the ships of war with their stout crews,
And bear aboard fresh water, furniture
Of war, much lesser victual, sallets, fruit,
All manner equipment for the squadron, sails,
Long spars.
           Also was chaffering on the Hoe,
Buying and bargaining, taking of leave
With tears and kisses, while on all hands pushed

Tall lusty men with baskets on their heads
Piled of fresh bread, and biscuit newly drawn.

Then shouts, 'The captains!'
                              Raleigh, Hawkins, Drake,
Old Martin Frobisher, and many more;
Howard, the Lord High Admiral, headed them —
They coming leisurely from the bowling green,
Elbowed their way.   For in their stoutness loth
To hurry when ill news first brake on them,
They playing a match ashore — ill news I say,
'The Spaniards are toward' — while panic-struck
The people ran about them, Drake cries out,
Knowing their fear should make the danger worse,
• 'Spaniards, my masters!   Let the Spaniards wait.
Fall not a-shouting for the boats; is time
To play the match out, ay to win, and then
To beat the Spaniards.'·
                              So the rest gave way
At his insistance, playing that afternoon
The bravest match (one saith) was ever scored.

'T was no time lost; nay, not a moment lost:
For look you, when the winning cast was made,
The town was calm, the anchors were all up,
The boats were manned to row them each to his ship,
The lowering cloud in the offing had gone south

Against the wind, and all was work, stir, heed,
Nothing forgot, nor grudged, nor slurred, and most
Men easy at heart as those brave sailors seemed.

And specially the women had put by
On a sudden their deep dread; yon Cornish coast
Neared of his insolency by the foe,
With his high seacastles numerous, seaforts
Many, his galleys out of number, manned
Each by three hundred slaves chained to the oar;
All his strong fleet of lesser ships, but great
As any of ours — why that same Cornish coast
Might have lain farther than the far west land,
So had a few stout-hearted looks and words
Wasted the meaning, chilled the menace of
That frightful danger, imminent, hard at hand.

'The captains come, the captains!' and I turned
As they drew on.   I marked the urgency
Flashing in each man's eye: fain to be forth
But willing to be held at leisure.   Then
Cried a fair woman of the better sort
To Howard, passing by her pannier'd ass.
'Apples, Lord Admiral, good captains all,
Look you, red apples sharp and sweet are these.'

Quoth he a little chafed, 'Let be, let be,
No time is this for bargaining, good dame.

Let be ; ' and pushing past, ' Beshrew thy heart
(And mine that I should say it), bargain ! nay.
I meant not bargaining,' she falters ; crying,
' I brought them my poor gift. Pray you now take,
Pray you.'
        He stops, and with a childlike smile
That makes the dame amend, stoops down to choose,
While I step up that love not many words,
' What should he do,' quoth I, ' to help this need
That hath a bag of money, and good will ? '
' Charter a ship,' he saith, nor e'er looks up,
' And put aboard her victual, tackle, shot,
Ought he can lay his hand on — look he give
Wide sea room to the Spanish hounds, make sail
For ships of ours, to ease of wounded men,
And succour with that freight he brings withal.'

His foot, yet speaking, was aboard his boat,
His comrades, each red apples in the hand,
Come after, and with blessings manifold
Cheering, and cries, ' Good luck, good luck ! ' they speed.

'T was three years three months past.
                O yet methinks
I hear that thunder crash i' the offing ; hear
Their words who when the crowd melted away
Gathered together. Comrades we of old,
About to adventure us at Howard's hest

On the unsafe sea.   For he, a Catholic,
As is my wife, and therefore my one child,
Detested and defied th' most Catholic King
Philip.   He, trusted of her grace — and cause
She had, the nation following suit — he deemed,
'T was whisper'd, ay and Raleigh, and Francis Drake
No less, the event of battle doubtfuller   •
Than English tongue might own ; the peril dread
As ought in this world ever can be deemed
That is not yet past praying for.
                                So far
So good.   As birds awaked do stretch their wings
The ships did stretch forth sail, full clad they towered
And right into the sunset went, hull down
E'en with the sun.
                        To us in twilight left,
Glory being over, came despondent thought
That mocked men's eager act.   From many a hill,
As if the land complained to Heaven, they sent
A towering shaft of murky incense high,
Livid with black despair in lieu of praise.
The green wood hissed at every beacon's edge
That widen'd fear.   The smell of pitchpots fled
Far over the field, and tongues of fire leaped up,
Ay, till all England woke, and knew, and wailed.

But we i' the night through that detested reek
Rode eastward.   Every mariner's voice was given

'Gainst any fear for the western shires. The cry
Was all, 'They sail for Calais roads, and thence,
The goal is London.'
          Nought slept, man nor beast.
Ravens and rooks flew forth, and with black wings,
Affrighted, swept our eyes. Pale eddying moths
Came by in crowds and whirled them on the flames.

We rode till pierced those beacon fires the shafts
O' the sun, and their red smouldering ashes dulled.
Beside them, scorched, smoke-blackened, weary, leaned
Men that had fed them, dropped their tired arms
And dozed.
        And also through that day we rode,
Till reapers at their nooning sat awhile
On the shady side of corn-shocks: all the talk
Of high, of low, or them that went or stayed
Determined but unhopeful; desperate
To strike a blow for England ere she fell.

And ever loomed the Spaniard to our thought,
Still waxed the fame of that great Armament —
New horsemen joining, swelled it more and more —
Their bulky ship galleons having five decks,
Zabraes, pataches, galleys of Portugal,
Caravels rowed with oars, their galliasses
Vast, and complete with chapels, chambers, towers.

And in the said ships of free mariners
Eight thousand, and of slaves two thousand more,
An army twenty thousand strong.   O then
Of culverin, of double culverin,
Ordnance and arms, all furniture of war,
Victual, and last their fierceness and great spleen,
Willing to founder, burn, split, wreck themselves,
But they would land, fight, overcome, and reign.

Then would we count up England.   Set by theirs,
Her fleet as walnut shells.   And a few pikes
Stored in the belfries, and a few brave men
For wielding them.   But as the morning wore,
And we went ever eastward, ever on,
Poured forth, poured down, a marching multitude
With stir about the towns ; and waggons rolled
With offerings for the army and the fleet.
Then to our hearts valour crept home again,
The loathèd name of Alva fanning it ;
Alva who did convert from our old faith
With many a black deed done for a white cause
(So spake they erewhile to it dedicate)
Them whom not death could change, nor fire, nor sword,
To thirst for his undoing.

Ay, as I am a Christian man, our thirst
Was comparable with Queen Mary's.   All

The talk was of confounding heretics,
The heretics the Spaniards. Yet methought,
'O their great multitude! Not harbour room
On our long coast for that great multitude.
They land — for who can let them — give us battle,
And after give us burial. Who but they,
For he that liveth shall be flying north
To bear off wife and child. Our very graves
Shall Spaniards dig, and in the daisied grass
Trample them down.'
            Ay, whoso will be brave,
Let him be brave beforehand. After th' event
If by good pleasure of God it go as then
He shall be brave an' liketh him. I say
Was no man but that deadly peril feared.

Nights riding two. Scant rest. Days riding three,
Then Foulkstone. Need is none to tell all forth
The gathering stores and men, the charter'd ship
That I, with two, my friends, got ready for sea.
Ready she was, so many another, small
But nimble ; and we sailing hugged the shore,
Scarce venturing out, so Drake had willed, a league,
And running westward aye as best we might,
When suddenly — behold them !
            On they rocked,
Majestical, slow, sailing with the wind.
O such a sight ! O such a sight, mine eyes,

Never shall you see more !

     In crescent form,
A vasty crescent nigh two leagues across
From horn to horn, the lesser ships within,
The great without, they did bestride as 't were
And make a township on the narrow seas.

It was about the point of dawn : and light.
All grey the sea, and ghostly grey the ships ;
And after in the offing rocked our fleet,
Having lain quiet in the summer dark.

O then methought, ' Flash, blessed gold of dawn,
And touch the topsails of our Admiral,
That he may after guide an emulous flock,
Old England's innocent white bleating lambs.
Let Spain within a pike's length hear them bleat,
Delivering of their pretty talk in a tongue
Whose meaning cries not for interpreter.'

And while I spoke, their topsails, friend and foe,
Glittered — and there was noise of guns ; pale smoke
Lagged after, curdling on the sun-fleck'd main.
And after that ? What after that, my soul ?
Who ever saw weakling white butterflies
Chasing of gallant swans, and charging them,
And spitting at them long red streaks of flame ?

We saw the ships of England even so
As in my vaunting wish that mocked itself
With 'Fool, O fool, to brag at the edge of loss.'
We saw the ships of England even so
Run at the Spaniards on a wind, lay to,
Bespatter them with hail of battle, then
Take their prerogative of nimble steerage,
Fly off, and ere the enemy, heavy in hand,
Delivered his reply to the wasteful wave
That made its grave of foam, race out of range,
Then tack and crowd all sail, and after them
Again.
   So harass'd they that mighty foe,
Moving in all its bravery to the east.
And some were fine with pictures of the saints,
Angels with flying hair and peakèd wings,
And high red crosses wrought upon their sails ;
From every mast brave flag or ensign flew,
And their long silken pennons serpented
Loose to the morning.   And the galley slaves,
Albeit their chains did clink, sang at the oar.

The sea was striped e'en like a tiger skin
With wide ship wakes.   .
       And many cried, amazed,
' What means their patience ? '
         ' Lo you,' others said,
' They pay with fear for their great costliness.

Some of their costliest needs must other guard;
Once guarded and in port look to yourselves,
They count one hundred and fifty. It behoves
Better they suffer this long running fight —
Better for them than that they give us battle,
And so delay the shelter of their roads.

'Two of their caravels we sank, and one
(Fouled with her consort in the rigging) took
Ere she could catch the wind when she rode free.
And we have riddled many a sail, and split
Of spars a score or two. What then? To-morrow
They look to straddle across the strait, and hold —
Having aye Calais for a shelter — hold
Our ships in fight. To-morrow shall give account
For our to-day. They will not we pass north
To meddle with Parma's flotilla; their hope
Being Parma, and a convoy they would be
For his flat boats that bode invasion to us;
And if he reach to London — ruin, defeat.'

Three fleets the sun went down on, theirs of fame
Th' Armada. After space old England's few;
And after that our dancing cockle-shells,
The volunteers. They took some pride in us,
For we were nimble, and we brought them powder,
Shot, weapons. They were short of these. Ill found,
Ill found. The bitter fruit of evil thrift.

But while obsequious, darting here and there,
We took their messages from ship to ship,
From ship to shore, the moving majesties
Made Calais Roads, cast anchor, all their less
In the middle ward; their greater ships outside
Impregnable castles fearing not assault.

So did we read their thought, and read it wrong,
While after the running fight we rode at ease,
For many (as is the way of Englishmen)
Having made light of our stout deeds, and light
O' the effects proceeding, saw these spread
To view. The Spanish Admiral's mighty host,
Albeit not broken, harass'd.
                                    Some did tow
Others that we had plagued, disabled, rent ;
Many full heavily damaged made their berths.

Then did the English anchor out of range.
To close was not their wisdom with such foe,
Rather to chase him, following in the rear.
Ay, truly they were giants in our eyes
And in our own. They took scant heed of us,
And we looked on, and knew not what to think,
Only that we were lost men, a lost Isle,
In every Spaniard's mind, both great and small.

But no such thought had place in Howard's soul,
And when 't was dark, and all their sails were furled,

When the wind veered a few points to the west,
And the tide turned ruffling along the roads,
He sent eight fireships forging down to them.

Terrible! Terrible!
             Blood-red pillars of reek
They looked on that vast host and troubled it,
As on th' Egyptian host One looked of old.

Then all the heavens were rent with a great cry,
The red avengers went right on, right on,
For none could let them; then was ruin, reek, flame;
Against th' unwieldy huge leviathans
They drave, they fell upon them as wild beasts,
And all together they did plunge and grind,
Their reefed sails set a-blazing. these flew loose
And forth like banners of destruction sped.
It was to look on as the body of hell
Seething; and some, their cables cut, ran foul
Of one the other, while the ruddy fire
Sped on aloft. One ship was stranded. One
Foundered, and went down burning; all the sea
Red as an angry sunset was made fell
With smoke and blazing spars that rode upright,
For as the fireships burst they scattered forth
Full dangerous wreckage. All the sky they scored
With flying sails and rocking masts, and yards
Licked of long flames. And flitting tinder sank

In eddies on the plagued mixed mob of ships
That cared no more for harbour, and were fain
At any hazard to be forth, and leave
Their berths in the blood-red haze.

It was at twelve
O' the clock when this fell out, for as the eight
Were towed, and left upon the friendly tide
To stalk like evil angels over the deep
And stare upon the Spaniards, we did hear
Their midnight bells.   It was at morning dawn
After our mariners thus had harried them
I looked my last upon their fleet, — and all,
That night had cut their cables, put to sea,
And scattering wide towards the Flemish coast
Did seem to make for Groveline.

As for us,
The captains told us off to wait on them,
Bearers of wounded enemies and friends,
Bearers of messages, bearers of store.

We saw not ought, but heard enough : we heard
(And God be thanked) of that long scattering chase
And driving of Sidonia from his hope,
Parma, who could not ought without his ships
And looked for them to break the Dutch blockade,
He meanwhile chafing lion-like in his lair.
We heard — and he — for all one summer day,
Fenning and Drake and Raynor, Fenton, Cross,

And more, by Greveline, where they once again
Did get the wind o' the Spaniards, noise of guns.
For coming with the wind, wielding themselves
Which way they listed (while in close array
The Spaniards stood but on defence), our own
Went at them, charged them high and charged them sore,
And gave them broadside after broadside.   Ay,
Till all the shot was spent both great and small.
It failed ; and in regard of that same want
They thought it not convenient to pursue
Their vessels farther.

      They were huge withal.
And might not be encounter'd one to one,
But close conjoined they fought, and poured great store
Of ordnance at our ships, though many of theirs,
Shot thorow and thorow, scarce might keep afloat.

Many were captured fighting, many sank.
This news they brought returned perforce, and left
The Spaniards forging north.   Themselves did watch
The river mouth, till Howard, his new store
Gathered, encounter coveting, once more
Made after them with Drake.

      And lo ! the wind
Got up to help us.   He yet flying north
(Their doughty Admiral) made all his wake
To smoke, and would not end to fight, but strewed
The ocean with his wreckage.   And the wind

Drave him before it, and the storm was fell,
And he went up to th' uncouth northern sea.

There did our mariners leave him.   Then did joy
Run like a sunbeam over the land, and joy
Rule in the stout heart of a regnant Queen.

But now the counsel came, 'Every man home,
For after Scotland rounded, when he curves
Southward, and all the batter'd armament,
What hinders on our undefended coast
To land where'er he listeth ?   Every man
Home.'
          And we mounted and did open forth
Like a great fan, to east. to north, to west,
And rumour met us flying, filtering
Down through the border.   News of wicked joy,
The wreckers rich in the Faroes, and the Isles
Orkney, and all the clansmen full of gear
Gathered from helpless mariners tempted in
To their undoing ; while a treacherous crew
Let the storm work upon their lives its will,
Spoiled them and gathered all their riches up.
Then did they meet like fate from Irish kernes,
Who dealt with them according to their wont.

In a great storm of wind that tore green leaves
And dashed them wet upon me, came I home.

Then greeted me my dame, and Rosamund,
Our one dear child, the heir of these my fields —
That I should sigh to think it !   There, no more.

Being right weary I betook me straight
To longed-for sleep, and I did dream and dream
Through all that dolourous storm; though noise of guns
Daunted the country in the moonless night,
Yet sank I deep and deeper in the dream
And took my fill of rest.
                                        A voice, a touch,
'Wake.'   Lo! my wife beside me, her wet hair
She wrung with her wet hands, and cried, 'A ship!
I have been down the beach.   O pitiful!
A Spanish ship ashore between the rocks,
And none to guide our people.   Wake.'
                                                    Then I
Raised on mine elbow looked; it was high day;
In the windy pother seas came in like smoke
That blew among the trees as fine small rain,
And then the broken water sun-besprent
Glitter'd, fell back and showed her high and fast
A caravel, a pinnace that methought
To some great ship had longed; her hap alone
Of all that multitude it was to drive
Between this land of England her right foe,
And that most cruel, where (for all their faith
Was one) no drop of water mote they drink

For love of God nor love of gold.

       I rose
And hasted ; I was soon among the folk,
But late for work. The crew, spent, faint, and bruised,
Saved for the most part of our men, lay prone
In grass, and women served them bread and mead,
Other the sea laid decently alone
Ready for burial. And a litter stood
In shade. Upon it lying a goodly man,
The govourner or the captain as it seemed,
Dead in his stiff gold-broider'd bravery,
And epaulet and sword. They must have loved
That man, for many had died to bring him in,
Their boats stove in were stranded here and there.
In one — but how I know not — brought they him,
And he was laid upon a folded flag,
Many times doubled for his greater ease,
That was our thought — and we made signs to them
He should have sepulture. But when they knew
They must needs leave him, for some marched them off
For more safe custody, they made great moan.

After, with two my neighbours drawing nigh,
One of them touched the Spaniard's hand and said,
' Dead is he but not cold ; ' the other then,
' Nay in good truth methinks he be not dead.'
Again the first, ' An' if he breatheth yet
He lies at his last gasp.' And this went off,

And left us two, that by the litter stayed,
Looking on one another, and we looked
(For neither willed to speak), and yet looked on.
Then would he have me know the meet was fixed
For nine o' the clock, and to be brief with you
He left me.   And I had the Spaniard home.
What other could be done?   I had him home.
Men on his litter bare him, set him down
In a fair chamber that was nigh the hall.

And yet he waked not from his deathly swoon,
Albeit my wife did try her skill, and now
Bad lay him on a bed, when lo the folds
Of that great ensign covered store of gold,
Rich Spanish ducats, raiment, Moorish blades
Chased in right goodly wise, and missals rare,
And other gear.   I locked it for my part
Into an armoury, and that fair flag
(While we did talk full low till he should end)
Spread over him.   Methought, the man shall die
Under his country's colours ; he was brave,
His deadly wound to that doth testify.

And when 't was seemly order'd, Rosamund,
My daughter, who had looked not yet on death,
Came in, a face all marvel, pity, and dread —
Lying against her shoulder sword-long flowers,
White hollyhocks to cross upon his breast.

Slowly she turned as of that sight afeard,
But while with daunted heart she moved anigh,
His eyelids quiver'd, quiver'd then the lip,
And he, reviving, with a sob looked up
And set on her the midnight of his eyes.

Then she, in act to place the burial gift
Bending above him, and her flaxen hair
Fall'n to her hand, drew back and stood upright
Comely and tall, her innocent fair face
Cover'd with blushes more of joy than shame.
' Father,' she cried, ' O father, I am glad.
Look you! the enemy liveth.'   ' 'T is enough,
My maiden,' quoth her mother, ' thou may'st forth,
But say an Avè first for him with me.'

Then they with hands upright at foot o' his bed
Knelt, his dark dying eyes at gaze on them,
Till as I think for wonder at them, more
Than for his proper strength, he could not die.

So in obedient wise my daughter risen,
And going, let a smile of comforting cheer
Lift her sweet lip, and that was all of her
For many a night and day that he beheld.

And then withal my dame, a leech of skill,
Tended the Spaniard fain to heal his wound,
Her women aiding at their best.   And he

'Twixt life and death awaken'd in the night
Full oft in his own tongue would make his moan,
And when he whisper'd any word I knew,
If I was present, for to pleasure him,
Then made I repetition of the same.
'Cordova,' quoth he faintly, 'Cordova,'
'T was the first word he mutter'd. 'Ay, we know,'
Quoth I, ' the stoutness of that fight ye made
Against the Moors and their Mahometry,
And dispossess'd the men of fame, the fierce
Khalifs of Cordova — thy home belike,
Thy city. A fair city Cordova.'

Then after many days, while his wound healed,
He with abundant seemly sign set forth
His thanks, but as for language had we none,
And oft he strove and failed to let us know
Some wish he had, but could not, so a week,
Two weeks went by. Then Rosamund my girl,
Hearing her mother plain on this, she saith,
'So please you, madam, show the enemy
A Psalter in our English tongue, and fetch
And give him that same book my father found
Wrapped in the ensign. Are they not the same
Those holy words? The Spaniard being devout,
He needs must know them.'

                    'Peace, thou pretty fool!
Is this a time to teach an alien tongue?'

Her mother made for answer. 'He is sick,
The Spaniard.' 'Cry you mercy,' quoth my girl,
'But I did think 't were easy to let show
How both the Psalters are of meaning like;
If he know Latin, and 't is like he doth,
So might he choose a verse to tell his thought.'

Then said I (ay, I did!) 'The girl shall try,'
And straight I took her to the Spaniard's side,
And he, admiring at her, all his face
Changed to a joy that almost showed as fear,
So innocent holy she did look, so grave
Her pitiful eyes.
        She sat beside his bed,
He covered with the ensign yet; and took
And showed the Psalters both, and she did speak
Her English words, but gazing was enough
For him at her sweet dimple, her blue eyes
That shone, her English blushes. Rosamund,
My beautiful dear child. He did but gaze,
And not perceive her meaning till she touched
His hand, and in her Psalter showed the word.

Then was all light to him; he laughed for joy,
And took the Latin Missal. O full soon,
Alas, how soon. one read the other's thought!
Before she left him, she had learned his name
Alonzo, told him hers, and found the care

Made night and day uneasy — Cordova,
There dwelt his father, there his kin, nor knew
Whether he lived or died, whether in thrall
To the Islanders for lack of ransom pined
Or rued the galling yoke of slavery.

So did he cast him on our kindness.   I —
And care not who may know it — I was kind,
And for that our stout Queen did think foul scorn
To kill the Spanish prisoners, and to guard
So many could not, liefer being to rid
Our country of them than to spite their own,
I made him as I might that matter learn,
Eking scant Latin with my daughter's wit,
And told him men let forth and driven forth
Did crowd our harbours for the ports of Spain,
By one of whom, he, with good aid of mine,
Should let his tidings go, and I plucked forth
His ducats that a meet reward might be.
Then he, the water standing in his eyes,
Made old King David's words due thanks convey.

Then Rosamund, this all made plain, arose
And curtsey'd to the Spaniard.   Ah, methinks
I yet behold her, gracious, innocent,
And flaxen-haired, and blushing maidenly,
When turning she retired, and his black eyes,
That hunger'd after her, did follow on;

And I bethought me, 'Thou shalt see no more,
Thou goodly enemy, my one ewe lamb.'

O, I would make short work of this. The wound
Healed, and the Spaniard rose, then could he stand,
And then about his chamber walk at ease.

Now we had counsell'd how to have him home,
And that same trading vessel beating up
The Irish Channel at my will, that same
I charter'd for to serve me in the war,
Next was I minded should mine enemy
Deliver to his father, and his land.
Daily we looked for her, till in our cove,
Upon that morn when first the Spaniard walked,
Behold her rocking ; and I hasted down
And left him waiting in the house.
                                        Woe 's me !
All being ready speed I home, and lo
My Rosamund, that by the Spaniard sat
Upon a cushion'd settle, book in hand.
I needs must think how in the deep alcove
Thick chequer'd shadows of the window-glass
Did fall across her kirtle and her locks,
For I did see her thus no more.
                                        She held
Her Psalter, and he his, and slowly read
Till he would stop her at the needed word.
'O well is thee,' she read, my Rosamund,

' O well is thee, and happy shalt thou be.
Thy wife — ' and there he stopped her, and he took
And kissed her hand, and show'd in 's own a ring,
Taking no heed of me, no heed at all.

Then I burst forth, the choler red i' my face
When I did see her blush, and put it on.
' Give me,' quoth I, and Rosamund, afraid,
Gave me the ring. I set my heel on it,
Crushed it, and sent the rubies scattering forth,
And did in righteous anger storm at him.
' What! what!' quoth I, ' before her father's eyes,
Thou universal villain, thou ingrate,
Thou enemy whom I shelter'd, fed, restored,
Most basest of mankind!' And Rosamund,
Arisen, her forehead pressed against mine arm,
And ' Father,' cries she, ' father.'

                              And I stormed
At him, while in his Spanish he replied
As one would speak me fair. ' Thou Spanish hound!'
' Father,' she pleaded. ' Alien vile,' quoth I,
' Plucked from the death, wilt thou repay me thus?
It is but three times thou hast set thine eyes
On this my daughter.' ' Father,' moans my girl;
And I, not willing to be so withstood,
Spoke roughly to her. Then the Spaniard's eyes
Blazed — then he stormed at me in his own tongue,
And all his Spanish arrogance and pride

Broke witless on my wrathful English.   Then
He let me know, for I perceived it well,
He reckon'd him mine equal, thought foul scorn
Of my displeasure, and was wroth with me
As I with him.   'Father,' sighed Rosamund.
'Go, get thee to thy mother, girl,' quoth I.
And slowly, slowly, she betook herself
Down the long hall; in lowly wise she went
And made her moans.

            But when my girl was gone
I stood at fault, th' occasion master'd me;
Belike it master'd him, for both felt mute.
I calmed me, and he calmed him as he might,
For I bethought me I was yet an host,
And he bethought him on the worthiness
Of my first deeds.

            So made I sign to him.
The tide was up, and soon I had him forth,
Delivered him his goods, commended him
To the captain o' the vessel, then plucked off
My hat, in seemly fashion taking leave,
And he was not outdone, but every way
Gave me respect, and on the deck we two
Parted, as I did hope, to meet no more.

Alas! my Rosamund, my Rosamund!
She did not weep, no.   Plain upon me, no.
Her eyes mote well have lost the trick of tears:

As new-washed flowers shake off the down-dropt rain,
And make denial of it, yet more blue
And fair of favour afterward, so they.
The wild woodrose was not more fresh of blee
Than her soft dimpled cheek : but I beheld,
Come home, a token hung about her neck,
Sparkling upon her bosom for his sake,
Her love, the Spaniard, she denied it not,
All unaware, good sooth, such love was bale.

And all that day went like another day,
Ay, all the next; then was I glad at heart ;
Methought, ' I am glad thou wilt not waste thy youth
Upon an alien man, mine enemy,
Thy nation's enemy. In truth, in truth,
This likes me very well. My most dear child,
Forget you grave dark mariner. The Lord
Everlasting,' I besought, ' bring it to pass.'

Stealeth a darker day within my hall,
A winter day of wind and driving foam.
They tell me that my girl is sick — and yet
Not very sick. I may not hour by hour,
More than one watching of a moon that wanes,
Make chronicle of change. A parlous change
When he looks back to that same moon at full.

Ah! ah! methought, 't will pass. It did not pass,
Though never she made moan. I saw the rings

Drop from her small white wasted hand.   And I,
Her father, tamed of grief, I would have given
My land, my name to have her as of old.
Ay, Rosamund I speak of with the small
White face.   Ay, Rosamund.   O near as white,
And mournfuller by much, her mother dear
Drooped by her couch; and while of hope and fear
Lifted or left, as by a changeful tide,
We thought 'The girl is better.' or we thought
'The girl will die,' that jewel from her neck
She drew, and prayed me send it to her love;
A token she was true e'en to the end.
What matter'd now?   But whom to send, and how
To reach the man?   I found an old poor priest,
Some peril 't was for him and me, she writ
My pretty Rosamund her heart's farewell,
She kissed the letter, and that old poor priest,
Who had eaten of my bread, and shelter'd him
Under my roof in troublous times, he took,
And to content her on this errand went,
While she as done with earth did wait the end.

Mankind bemoan them on the bitterness
Of death.   Nay, rather let them chide the grief
Of living, chide the waste of mother-love
For babes that joy to get away to God;
The waste of work and moil and thought and thrift
And father-love for sons that heed it not,

3

And daughters lost and gone. Ay, let them chide
These.   Yet I chide not.   That which I have done
Was rightly done; and what thereon befell
Could make no right a wrong, e'en were 't to do
Again.
       I will be brief.   The days drag on,
My soul forebodes her death, my lonely age.
Once I despondent in the moaning wood
Look out, and lo a caravel at sea,
A man that climbs the rock, and presently
The Spaniard!
       I did greet him, proud no more.
He had braved durance, as I knew, ay death,
To land on th' Island soil.   In broken words
Of English he did ask me how she fared.
Quoth I, 'She is dying, Spaniard; Rosamund
My girl will die;' but he is fain, saith he,
To talk with her, and all his mind to speak;
I answer, 'Ay, my whilome enemy,
But she is dying.'   'Nay, now nay,' quoth he,
'So be she liveth,' and he moved me yet
For answer; then quoth I, 'Come life, come death,
What thou wilt, say.'
       Soon made we Rosamund
Aware, she lying on the settle, wan
As a lily in the shade, and while she not
Believed for marvelling, comes he roundly in,
The tall grave Spaniard, and with but one smile,

One look of ruth upon her small pale face,
All slowly as with unaccustom'd mouth,
Betakes him to that English he hath conned,
Setting the words out plain :
                                      'Child! Rosamund!
Love! An so please thee, I would be thy man.
By all the saints will I be good to thee.
Come.'
        Come! what think you, would she come? Ay, ay.
They love us, but our love is not their life.
For the dark mariner's love lived Rosamund.
Soon for his kiss she bloomed, smiled for his smile.
(The Spaniard reaped e'en as th' Evangel saith,
And bore in 's bosom forth my golden sheaf.)
She loved her father and her mother well,
But loved the Spaniard better.   It was sad
To part, but she did part ; and it was far
To go, but she did go.   The priest was brought,
The ring was bless'd that bound my Rosamund,
She sailed, and I shall never see her more.

One soweth and another reapeth.   Ay,
Too true! too true!

ECHO AND THE FERRY.

A Y, Oliver! I was but seven, and he was eleven;
    He looked at me pouting and rosy. I blushed
    where I stood.
They had told us to play in the orchard (and I only seven!
A small guest at the farm); but he said, 'Oh, a girl was
    no good!'
So he whistled and went, he went over the stile to the
    wood.
It was sad, it was sorrowful! Only a girl — only seven!
At home in the dark London smoke I had not found it out.
The pear-trees looked on in their white, and blue birds
    flash'd about,
And they too were angry as Oliver. Were they eleven?
I thought so. Yes, everyone else was eleven — eleven!

So Oliver went, but the cowslips were tall at my feet,
And all the white orchard with fast-falling blossom was
    litter'd;
And under and over the branches those little birds
    twitter'd,
While hanging head downwards they scolded because I
    was seven.
A pity. A very great pity. One should be eleven.

But soon I was happy, the smell of the world was so sweet,
And I saw a round hole in an apple-tree rosy and old.
Then I knew! for I peeped, and I felt it was right they
    should scold!
Eggs small and eggs many. For gladness I broke into
    laughter;
And then some one else — oh, how softly! — came after,
    came after
With laughter — with laughter came after.

And no one was near us to utter that sweet mocking call,
That soon very tired sank low with a mystical fall.
But this was the country — perhaps it was close under
    heaven;
Oh, nothing so likely; the voice might have come from
    it even.
I knew about heaven. But this was the country, of this
Light, blossom, and piping, and flashing of wings not at all.
Not at all. No. But one little bird was an easy forgiver:
She peeped, she drew near as I moved from her domicile
    small,
Then flashed down her hole like a dart — like a dart from
    the quiver.
And I waded atween the long grasses and felt it was bliss.

— So this was the country; clear dazzle of azure and
    shiver
And whisper of leaves, and a humming all over the tall

White branches, a humming of bees.   And I came to the
   wall —
A little low wall — and looked over, and there was the
   river,
The lane that led on to the village, and then the sweet
   river
Clear shining and slow, she had far far to go from her
   snow ;
But each rush gleamed a sword in the sunlight to guard
   her long flow,
And she murmur'd, methought, with a speech very soft —
   very low.
'The ways will be long, but the days will be long,' quoth
   the river,
'To me a long liver, long, long ! ' quoth the river — the
   river.

I dreamed of the country that night, of the orchard, the
   sky,
The voice that had mocked coming after and over and
   under.
But at last — in a day or two namely — Eleven and I
Were very fast friends, and to him I confided the wonder.
He said that was Echo.   ' Was Echo a wise kind of bee
That had learned how to laugh : could it laugh in one's
   ear and then fly
And laugh again yonder ? ' ' No ; Echo ' — he whispered
   it low —

'Was a woman, they said, but a woman whom no one
     could see

And no one could find; and he did not believe it,
     not he,

But he could not get near for the river that held us
     asunder.

Yet I that had money — a shilling, a whole silver
     shilling —

We might cross if I thought I would spend it.' 'Oh yes,
     I was willing' —

And we ran hand in hand, we ran down to the ferry, the
     ferry,

And we heard how she mocked at the folk with a voice
     clear and merry

When they called for the ferry; but oh! she was very —
     was very

Swift-footed. She spoke and was gone; and when Oliver
     cried,

'Hie over! hie over! you man of the ferry — the ferry!'

By the still water's side she was heard far and wide — she
     replied

And she mocked in her voice sweet and merry, 'You man
     of the ferry,

You man of — you man of the ferry!'

'Hie over!' he shouted. The ferryman came at his
     calling,

Across the clear reed-border'd river he ferried us fast; —

Such a chase! Hand in hand, foot to foot, we ran on; it surpass'd

All measure her doubling — so close, then so far away falling,

Then gone, and no more. Oh! to see her but once unaware,

And the mouth that had mocked, but we might not (yet sure she was there!),

Nor behold her wild eyes and her mystical countenance fair.

We sought in the wood, and we found the wood-wren in her stead;

In the field, and we found but the cuckoo that talked overhead;

By the brook, and we found the reed-sparrow deep-nested, in brown —

Not Echo, fair Echo! for Echo, sweet Echo! was flown.

So we came to the place where the dead people wait till God call.

The church was among them, grey moss over roof, over wall,

Very silent, so low. And we stood on a green grassy mound

And looked in at a window, for Echo, perhaps, in her round

Might have come in to hide there. But no; every oak-carven seat

Was empty. We saw the great Bible — old, old, very
old,

And the parson's great Prayer-book beside it; we heard
the slow beat

Of the pendulum swing in the tower; we saw the clear
gold

Of a sunbeam float down to the aisle and then waver and
play

On the low chancel step and the railing, and Oliver
said,

' Look, Katie! look, Katie! when Lettice came here to
be wed

She stood where that sunbeam drops down, and all white
was her gown;

And she stepped upon flowers they strew'd for her.' Then
quoth small Seven:

' Shall I wear a white gown and have flowers to walk upon
ever ? '

All doubtful : ' It takes a long time to grow up,' quoth
Eleven ;

' You 're so little, you know, and the church is so old, it
can never

Last on till you 're tall.' And in whispers — because it
was old

And holy, and fraught with strange meaning, half felt,
but not told,

Full of old parsons' prayers, who were dead, of old days,
of old folk,

Neither heard nor beheld, but about us, in whispers we
    spoke.
Then we went from it softly and ran hand in hand to the
    strand,
While bleating of flocks and birds' piping made sweeter
    the land.
And Echo came back e'en as Oliver drew to the ferry,
'O Katie!' 'O Katie!' 'Come on, then!' 'Come on,
    then!' 'For, see,
The round sun, all red, lying low by the tree ' — ' by the
    tree.'
' By the tree.' Ay, she mocked him again, with her voice
    sweet and merry :
' Hie over !' ' Hie over !' ' You man of the ferry ' —
    ' the ferry.'
      ' You man of the ferry —
    You man of — you man of — the ferry.'

Ay, here — it was here that we woke her, the Echo of old ;
All life of that day seems an echo, and many times told.
Shall I cross by the ferry to-morrow, and come in my
    white
To that little low church ? and will Oliver meet me
    anon ?
Will it all seem an echo from childhood pass'd over —
    pass'd on ?
Will the grave parson bless us ? Hark, hark ! in the dim
    failing light

I hear her! As then the child's voice clear and high,
  sweet and merry

Now she mocks the man's tone with 'Hie over! Hie
  over the ferry!'

'And, Katie.' 'And, Katie.' 'Art out with the glow-
  worms to-night,

My Katie?' 'My Katie!' For gladness I break into
  laughter

And tears. Then it all comes again as from far-away
  years;

Again, some one else — oh, how softly! — with laughter
  comes after,

   Comes after — with laughter comes after.

PRELUDES TO A PENNY READING.

A Schoolroom.

SCHOOLMASTER (*not certificated*), VICAR, *and* CHILD.

VICAR. Why did you send for me? I hope all 's
  right?

Schoolmaster. Well, sir, we thought this end o' the room
  was dark.

V. Indeed! So 't is. There 's my new study lamp —

S. 'T would stand, sir, well beside yon laurel wreath.
Shall I go fetch it?

V.   Do, we must not fail.
Bring candles also.

[*Exit Schoolmaster.   Vicar arranges chairs.*

                        Now, small six years old,
And why may you be here?
    Child.   I 'm helping father ;
But, father, why d' you take such pains ?
    V.   Sweet soul,
That 's what I 'm for !
    C.   What, and for nothing else ?
    V. Yes!   I 'm to bring thee up to be a man.
    C. And what am I for ?
    V.   There, I 'm busy now.
    C. Am I to bring you up to be a child ?
    V. Perhaps!   Indeed, I have heard it said thou art.
    C. Then when may I begin ?
    V.   I 'm busy, I say.
Begin to-morrow an thou canst, my son,
And mind to do it well.   [*Exit Vicar and Child.*

    Enter a group of women, and some children.

Mrs. Thorpe.   Fine lot o' lights !
Mrs. Jillifer. Should be !   Would folk put on their
        Sunday best
I' the week unless they looked to have it seen ?
What, you here, neighbour !
    Mrs. Smith.   Ay, you may say that.
Old Madam called ; said she, 'My son would feel

So sorry if you did not come,' and slipped
The penny in my hand, she did; said I,
' Ma'am, that 's not it. In short, some say your last
Was worth the penny and more. I know a man,
A sober man, who said, and stuck to it,
Worth a good twopence. But I 'm strange, I 'm shy.'
' We hope you 'll come for once,' said she. In short,
I said I would to oblige 'em.

   Mrs. Green.   Ah, 't was well.

   Mrs. S. But I feel strange, and music gets i' my throat,
It always did. And singers be so smart,
Ladies and folk from other parishes,
Candles and cheering, greens and flowers and all
I was not used to such in my young day ;
We kept ourselves at home.

   Mrs. J.   Never say ' used,'
The most of us have many a thing to do
We were not used to. If you come to that,
Why none of us are used to growing old,
It takes us by surprise, as one may say,
That work, when we begin 't, and yet 't is work
That all of us must do.

   Mrs. G.   Nay, nay, not all.

   Mrs. J. I ask your pardon, neighbour ; you be right,
Not all.

   Mrs. G. And my sweet maid scarce three months dead.

   Mrs. J. I ask your pardon truly.

   Mrs. G.   No, my dear,

Thou 'lt never see old days. I cannot stint
To fret, the maiden was but twelve years old,
So toward, such a scholar.

  Mrs. S.   Ay, when God,
That knows, comes down to choose, He 'll take the best.

  Mrs. T. But I 'm right glad you came, it pleases
   them.

My son, that loves his book, ' Mother,' said he,
' Go to the Reading when you have a chance,
For there you get a change, and you see life.'
But Reading or no Reading, I am slow
To learn.   When parson after comes his rounds,
' Did it,' to ask with a persuading smile,
' Open your mind? ' the woman doth not live
Feels more a fool.

  Mrs. J.   I always tell him ' Yes,'
For he means well.   Ay, and I like the songs.
Have you heard say what they shall read to-night?

  Mrs. S. Neighbour, I hear 't is something of the East.
But what, I ask you, is the East to us,
And where d' ye think it lies ?

  Mrs. J.   The children know,
At least they say they do ; there 's nothing deep
Nor nothing strange but they get hold on it.

  Enter Schoolmaster and a dozen children.

  S Now ladies, ladies, you must please to sit
More close ; the room fills fast, and all these lads

And maidens either have to sing before
The Reading, or else after. By your leave
I 'll have them in the front, I want them here.
[*The women make room.*

Enter ploughmen, villagers, servants, and children.

And mark me, boys, if I hear cracking o' nuts,
Or see you flicking acorns and what not
While folks from other parishes observe,
You 'll hear on it when you don't look to.   Tom
And Jemmy and Roger, sing as loud 's ye can,
Sing as the maidens do, are they afraid ?
And now I 'm stationed handy facing you,
Friends all, I 'll drop a word by your good leave.
   Young ploughman. Do, master, do, we like your words
     a vast.
Though there be nought to back 'em up, ye see,
As when we were smaller.
   S.   Mark me, then, my lads.
When Lady Laura sang, ' I don't think much,'
Says her fine coachman. ' of your manners here.
We drove eleven miles in the dark, it rained,
And ruts in your cross roads are deep. We 're here,
My lady sings, they sit all open-mouthed,
And when she 's done they never give one cheer.'
   Old man. Be folks to clap if they don't like the song ?
   S. Certain, for manners.

Enter VICAR, *wife, various friends with violins and a flute.*
They come to a piano, and one begins softly to tune his
violin, while the Vicar speaks.

V. Friends, since there is a place where you must hear
When I stand up to speak, I would not now
If there were any other found to bid
You welcome. Welcome, then; these with me ask
No better than to please, and in good sooth
I ever find you willing to be pleased.
When I demand not more, but when we fain
Would lead you to some knowledge fresh, and ask
Your careful heed, I hear that some of you
Have said, 'What good to know, what good to us?
He puts us all to school, and our school days
Should be at end. Nay, if they needs must teach,
Then let them teach us what shall mend our lot;
The laws are strict on us, the world is hard.'
You friends and neighbours, may I dare to speak?
I know the laws are strict, and the world hard,
For ever will the world help that man up
That is already coming up, and still
And ever help him down that 's going down.
Yet say, 'I will take the words out of thy mouth,
O world, being yet more strict with mine own life.
Thou law, to gaze shall not be worth thy while
On whom beyond thy power doth rule himself.'
Yet seek to know, for whoso seek to know

They seek to rise, and best they mend their lot.
Methinks, if Adam and Eve in their garden days
Had scorned the serpent, and obediently
Continued God's good children, He Himself
Had led them to the Tree of Knowledge soon
And bid them eat the fruit thereof, and yet
Not find it apples of death.

    Vicar's wife (aside).   Now, dearest John,
We're ready.   Lucky too! you always go
Above the people's heads.

Young farmer stands forward, Vicar presenting him.

SONG.

I.

Sparkle of snow and of frost,
    Blythe air and the joy of cold,
Their grace and good they have lost,
    As print o' her foot by the fold.
Let me back to yon desert sand,
    Rose-lipped love — from the fold,
Flower-fair girl — from the fold,
    Let me back to the sultry land.
The world is empty of cheer,
    Forlorn, forlorn, and forlorn,
As the night-owl's sob of fear,
    As Memnon moaning at morn.

4

For love of thee, my dear,
    I have lived a better man,
        O my Mary Anne,
        My Mary Anne.

II.

Away, away, and away,
    To an old palm-land of tombs,
Washed clear of our yesterday
    And where never a snowdrop blooms,
Nor wild becks talk as they go
    Of tender hope we had known,
Nor mosses of memory grow
    All over the wayside stone.

III.

Farewell, farewell, and farewell,
    As voice of a lover's sigh
In the wind let yon willow wave
    'Farewell, farewell, and farewell.'
The sparkling frost-stars brave
    On thy shrouded bosom lie;
Thou art gone apart to dwell,
    But I fain would have said good-bye.
        For love of thee in thy grave
        I have lived a better man,
            O my Mary Anne,
            My Mary Anne.

Mrs. Thorpe (aside). O hearts! why, what a song!
To think on it, and he a married man!
    Mrs. Jillifer (aside). Bless you, that makes for nothing,
      nothing at all,
They take no heed upon the words. His wife,
Look you, as pleased as may be, smiles on him.
    Mrs. T. (aside). Neighbours, there's one thing beats
      me. We've enough
O' trouble in the world; I 've cried my fill
Many and many a time by my own fire:
Now why, I 'll ask you, should it comfort me
And ease my heart when, pitiful and sweet,
One sings of other souls and how they mourned?
A body would have thought that did not know
Songs must be merry, full of feast and mirth,
Or else would all folk flee away from them.
    Mrs. S. (aside). 'T is strange, and I too ·love the sad
      ones best.
    Mrs. T. (aside). Ay, how they clap him! 'T is as who
      should say,
Sing! we were pleased; sing us another song;
As if they did not know he loves to sing.
Well may he, not an organ pipe they blow
On Sunday in the church is half so sweet;
But he 's a hard man.
    Mrs. J. (aside).   Mark me, neighbours all,
Hard though he be — ay, and the mistress hard —
If he do sing 't will be a sorrowful

Sad tale of sweethearts, that shall make you wish
Your own time would come over again, although
Were partings in 't and tears.   Hist ! now he sings.

Young farmer sings again.

'Come hither, come hither.'   The broom was in blossom
   all over yon rise ;
   There went a wide murmur of brown bees about it with
   songs from the wood.
'We shall never be younger !   O love, let us forth, for
   the world 'neath our eyes,
   Ay, the world is made young e'en as we, and right fair
   is her youth and right good.'

Then there fell the great yearning upon me, that never
   yet went into words ;
   While lovesome and moansome thereon spake and
   falter'd the dove to the dove.
And I came at her calling, ' Inherit, inherit, and sing with
   the birds ; '
   I went up to the wood with the child of my heart and
   the wife of my love.

O pure !   O pathetic !   Wild hyacinths drank it, the
   dream light, apace
   Not a leaf moved at all 'neath the blue, they hung
   waiting for messages kind ;

Tall cherry-trees dropped their white blossom that drifted
    no whit from its place,
  For the south very far out to sea had the lulling low
    voice of the wind.

And the child's dancing foot gave us part in the ravish-
    ment almost a pain,
  An infinite tremor of life, a fond murmur that cried out
    on time,
Ah short! must all end in the doing and spend itself
    sweetly in vain,
  And the promise be only fulfilment to lean from the
    height of its prime ?

'We shall never be younger;' nay, mock me not, fancy,
    none call from yon tree;
  They have thrown me the world they went over, went
    up, and, alas! for my part
I am left to grow old, and to grieve, and to change; but
    they change not with me;
  They will never be older, the child of my love, and the
    wife of my heart.

Mrs. J. I told you so!
Mrs. T. (*aside*).   That did you, neighbour. Ay,
Partings, said you, and tears: I liked the song.
  Mrs. G. Who be these coming to the front to sing ?

Mrs. J. (*aside*). Why, neighbour, these be sweethearts,
    so 't is said,
And there was much ado to make her sing ;
She would, and would not ; and he wanted her,
And, mayhap, wanted to be seen with her.
'T is Tomlin's pretty maid, his only one.
    Mrs. G. (*aside*). I did not know the maid, so fair she
      looks.
    Mrs. J. (*aside*). He 's a right proper man she has at
      last ;
Walks over many a mile (and counts them nought)
To court her after work hours, that he doth,
Not like her other — why, he 'd let his work
Go all to wrack, and lay it to his love,
While he would sit and look, and look and sigh.
Her father sent him to the right-about.
' If love,' said he, ' won't make a man of you,
Why, nothing will ! 'T is mainly that love 's for.
The right sort makes,' said he, ' a lad a man ;
The wrong sort makes,' said he, ' a man a fool.'

     Vicar presents a young man and a girl.

           DUET.

  She. While he dreams, mine old grand sire,
     And you red logs glow,
    Honey, whisper by the fire,
     Whisper, honey low.

He. Honey, high 's yon weary hill,
　　　Stiff 's yon weary loam ;
　　　Lacks the work o' my goodwill,
　　　Fain I 'd take thee home.
O how much longer, and longer, and longer,
　　An' how much longer shall the waiting last?
Berries red are grown, April birds are flown,
　　Martinmas gone over, ay, and harvest past.

She. Honey, bide, the time 's awry,
　　　Bide awhile, let be.
He. Take my wage then, lay it by,
　　　Till 't come back with thee.
　　　The red money, the white money,
　　　Both to thee I bring —
She. Bring ye ought beside, honey ?
He.　Honey, ay, the ring.

Duet. But how much longer, and longer, and longer,
　　O how much longer shall the waiting last?
Berries red are grown, April birds are flown,
　　Martinmas gone over, and the harvest past.
　　　　　　　　　　　　　　　[Applause.

　Mrs. S. (aside). O she 's a pretty maid, and sings so
　　small
And high, 't is like a flute. And she must blush
Till all her face is roses newly blown.
How folks do clap. She knows not where to look.

There now she 's off ; he standing like a man
To face them.

   Mrs. G. (*aside*).   Makes his bow, and after her ;
But what 's the good of clapping when they 're gone?

   Mrs. T. (*aside*).   Why 't is a London fashion as I 'm told,
And means they 'd have 'em back to sing again.

   Mrs. J. (*aside*).   Neighbours, look where her father,
      red as fire,
Sits pleased and 'shamed, smoothing his Sunday hat ;
And Parson bustles out.   Clap on, clap on.
Coming ? Not she ! There comes her sweetheart though.

     Vicar presents the young man again..

SONG.

I.

Rain clouds flew beyond the fell,
   No more did thunders lower,
Patter, patter, on the beck
   Dropt a clearing shower.
Eddying floats of creamy foam
   Flecked the waters brown,
As we rode up to cross the ford,
   Rode up from yonder town.
      Waiting on the weather,
      She and I together,
      Waiting on the weather,
        Till the flood went down.

The sun came out, the wet leaf shone,
  Dripped the wildwood vine.
Betide me well, betide me woe,
  That hour 's for ever mine.
With thee Mary, with thee Mary,
  Full oft I pace again,
Asleep, awake, up yonder glen,
  And hold thy bridle rein.
      Waiting on the weather,
      Thou and I together,
      Waiting on the weather,
        Till the flood shall wane.

III.

And who, though hope did come to nought,
  Would memory give away ?
I lighted down, she leaned full low,
  Nor chid that hour's delay.
With thee Mary, with thee Mary,
  Methought my life to crown,
But we ride up, but we ride up,
  No more from yonder town.
      Waiting on the weather,
      Thou and I together,
      Waiting on the weather,
        Till the flood go down.

Mrs. J. (aside). Well, very well; but what of fiddler
 Sam?

I ask you, neighbours, if 't be not his turn.

An honest man, and ever pays his score ;

Born in the parish, old, blind as a bat,

And strangers sing before him; 't is a shame !

Mrs. S. (aside). Ay, but his daughter —

Mrs. J. (aside).   Why, the maid 's a maid

One would not set to guide the chant in church,

But when she sings to earn her father's bread,

The mildest mother's son may cry ' Amen.'

Mrs. S. (aside). They say he plays not always true.

Mrs. J. (aside).   What then ?

Mrs. T. (aside). Here comes my lady. She 's too fat
 by half

For love songs. O! the lace upon her gown,

I wish I had the getting of it up,

'T would be a pretty penny in my ponch.

Mrs. J. (aside). Be quiet now for manners.

   Vicar presents a lady, who sings.

       •   I.

   Dark flocks of wildfowl riding out the storm
     Upon a pitching sea,
   Beyond grey rollers vex'd that rear and form,
   When piping winds urge on their destiny,
   To fall back ruined in white continually.

And I at our trysting stone,
Whereto I came down alone,
Was fain o' the wind's wild moan.
O, welcome were wrack and were rain
And beat of the battling main,
For the sake of love's sweet pain,
For the smile in two brown eyes,
For the love in any wise,
To bide though the last day dies;
For a hand on my wet hair,
For a kiss e'en yet I wear,
For — bonny Jock was there.

II.

Pale precipices while the sun lay low
　　Tinct faintly of the rose,
And mountain islands mirror'd in a flow,
Forgotten of all winds (their manifold
Peaks, reared into the glory and the glow),
　　Floated in purple and gold.
　　And I, o'er the rocks alone,
　　Of a shore all silent grown,
　　Came down to our trysting stone,
　　And sighed when the solemn ray
　　Paled in the wake o' the day.
　　'Wellaway, wellaway, —
　　Comfort is not by the shore,
　　Going the gold that it wore,

Purple and rose are no more,
World and waters are wan,
And night will be here anon,
And — bonny Jock 's gone.'
[*Moderate applause, and calls for fiddler Sam.*

Mrs. Jillifer (*aside*). Now, neighbours, call again and
be not shamed ;
Stand by the parish, and the parish folk,
Them that are poor.   I told you! here he comes.
Parson looks glum, but brings him and his girl.

The fiddler Sam plays, and his daughter sings.

Touch the sweet string.   Fly forth, my heart,
Upon the music like a bird ;
The silvery notes shall add their part,
And haply yet thou shalt be heard.
Touch the sweet string.

The youngest wren of nine
Dimpled, dark, and merry,
Brown her locks, and her two eyne
Browner than a berry.

When I was not in love
Maidens met I many ;
Under sun now walks but one,
Nor others mark I any.

Twin lambs, a mild-eyed ewe,
   That would her follow bleating,
A heifer white as snow
   I 'll give to my sweet sweeting.

Touch the sweet string. If yet too young,
   O love of loves, for this my song,
I 'll pray thee count it all unsung,
   And wait thy leisure, wait it long.
      Touch the sweet string.

                  [*Much applause.*

Vicar. You hear them, Sam. You needs must play again,
Your neighbours ask it.
   Fiddler.   Thank ye, neighbours all,
I have my feelings though I be but poor;
I 've tanged the fiddle here this forty year,
And I should know the trick on 't.

   The fiddler plays, and his daughter sings.

For Exmoor —
For Exmoor, where the red deer run, my weary heart
   doth cry.
She that will a rover wed, far her foot shall hie.
Narrow, narrow, shows the street, dull the narrow sky.
(*Buy my cherries, whiteheart cherries, good my masters,
   buy.*)

For Exmoor —
O he left me, left alone, aye to think and sigh,
'Lambs feed down yon sunny coombe, hind and yearling
    shy,
Mid the shrouding vapours walk now like ghosts on high.'
(*Buy my cherries, blackheart cherries, lads and lassies, buy.*)

For Exmoor —
Dear my dear, why did ye so? Evil days have I,
Mark no more the antler'd stag, hear the curlew cry.
Milking at my father's gate while he leans anigh.
(*Buy my cherries, whiteheart, blackheart, golden girls, O
    buy.*)

    Mrs. T. (*aside*). I 've known him play that Exmoor
        song afore.
Ah me! and I 'm from Exmoor. I could wish
To hear 't no more.
    Mrs. S. (*aside*). Neighbours, 't is mighty hot.
Ay, now they throw the window up, that 's well,
A body could not breathe.
               [*The fiddler and his daughter go away.*
    Mrs. Jillifer (*aside*). They 'll hear no parson's preach-
        ing, no not they!
But innocenter songs, I do allow,
They could not well have sung than these to-night.
That man knows just so well as if he saw
They were not welcome.

The Vicar stands up, on the point of beginning to read,
when the tuning and twang of the fiddle is heard close
outside the open window, and the daughter sings in a
clear cheerful voice. A little tittering is heard in the
room, and the Vicar pauses discomfited. .

I.

O my heart! what a coil is here !
Laurie, why will ye hold me dear ?
Laurie, Laurie, lad, make not wail,
With a wiser lass ye 'll sure prevail,
For ye sing like a woodland nightingale.
And there 's no sense in it under the sun ;
For of three that woo I can take but one,
So what 's to be done — what 's to be done ?
  And
There 's no sense in it under the sun.

II.

Hal, brave Hal, from your foreign parts
Come home you 'll choose among kinder hearts.
Forget, forget, you 're too good to hold
A fancy 't were best should faint, grow cold,
And fade like an August marigold ;
For of three that woo I can take but one,
And what 's to be done — what 's to be done ?

There 's no sense in it under the sun,
   And
Of three that woo I can take but one.

III.

Geordie, Geordie, I count you true,
Though language sweet I have none for you.
Nay, but take me home to the churning mill
When cherry boughs white on yon mounting hill
Hang over the tufts o' the daffodil.
For what 's to be done — what 's to be done?
Of three that woo I must e'en take one,
Or there 's no sense in it under the sun,
   And
What 's to be done — what 's to be done?.

V. (*aside*). What 's to be done, indeed!
Wife (*aside*).   Done! nothing, love.
Either the thing has done itself, or *they*
Must undo.   Did they call for fiddler Sam?
Well, now they have him.
      [*More tuning heard outside.*
Mrs. J. (*aside*). Live and let live 's my motto.
Mrs. T.   So 't is mine.
Who 's Sam, that he must fly in Parson's face?
He 's had his turn.   He never gave these lights,
Cut his best flowers —

Mrs. S. (aside). He takes no pride in us.
Speak up, good neighbour, get the window shut.
    Mrs. J. (rising). I ask your pardon truly, that I do —
La! but the window — there's a parlous draught;
The window punishes rheumatic folk —
We'd have it shut, sir.
    Others. Truly, that we would.
    V. Certainly, certainly, my friends, you shall.
    [*The window is shut, and the Reading begins amid
    marked attention.*

KISMET.

INTO the rock the road is cut full deep,
    At its low ledges village children play,
From its high rifts fountains of leafage weep,
    And silvery birches sway.

The boldest climbers have its face forsworn,
    Sheer as a wall it doth all daring flout;
But benchlike at its base, and weather-worn,
    A narrow ledge leans out.

There do they set forth feasts in dishes rude
    Wrought of the rush — wild strawberries on the bed
Left into August, apples brown and crude,
    Cress from the cold well-head.

5

Shy gamesome girls, small daring imps of boys,
　　But gentle, almost silent at their play —
Their fledgling daws, for food, make far more noise
　　　Ranged on the ledge than they.

The children and the purple martins share
　　(Loveliest of birds) possession of the place;
They veer and dart cream-breasted round the fair
　　　Faces with wild sweet grace.

Fresh haply from Palmyra desolate,
　　Palmyra pale in light and storyless —
From perching in old Tadmor mate by mate
　　　In the waste wilderness.

These know the world; what do the children know?
　　They know the woods, their groaning noises weird,
They climb in trees that overhang the slow
　　　Deep mill-stream, loved and feared.

Where shaken water-wheels go creak and clack,
　　List while a lorn thrush calls and almost speaks;
See willow-wrens with elderberries black
　　　Staining their slender beaks.

They know full well how squirrels spend the day;
　　They peeped when field-mice stole and stored the seed.
And voles along their under-water way
　　　Donned collars of bright beads.

Still from the deep-cut road they love to mark
 Where set, as in a frame, the nearer shapes
Rise out of hill and wood; then long downs dark
 As purple bloom on grapes.

But farms whereon the tall wheat musters goin,
 High barley whitening, creases in bare hills,
Reed-feathered, castle-like brown churches old,
 Nor churning water-mills,

Shall make ought seem so fair as that beyond —
 Beyond the down, which draws their fealty ;
Blow high, blow low, some hearts do aye respond
 The wind is from the sea.

Above the steep-cut steps as they did grow,
 The children's cottage homes embowered are seen ;
Were this a world unfallen, they scarce could show
 More beauteous red and green.

Milk-white and vestal-chaste the hollyhock
 Grows tall, clove, sweetgale nightly shed forth spice,
Long woodbines leaning over scent the rock
 With airs of Paradise.

Here comforted of pilot stars they lie
 In charmèd dreams, but not of wold nor lea.
Behold a ship ! her wide yards score the sky ;
 She sails a steel-blue sea.

As turns the great amassment of the tide,
　　Drawn of the silver despot to her throne,
So turn the destined souls, so far and wide
　　　　The strong deep claims its own.

Still the old tale; these dreaming islanders,
　　Each with hot Sunderbunds a somewhat owns
That calls, the grandsire's blood within them stirs
　　　　Dutch Java guards his bones.

And these were orphan'd when a leak was sprung
　　Far out from land when all the air was balm;
The shipmen saw their faces as they hung,
　　　　And sank in the glassy calm.

These, in an orange-sloop their father plied,
　　Deck-laden deep she sailed from Cadiz town,
A black squall rose, she turned upon her side,
　　　　Drank water and went down.

They too shall sail.　High names of alien lands
　　Are in the dream, great names their fathers knew;
Madras, the white surf rearing on her sands,
　　　　E'en they shall breast it too.

See threads of scarlet down fell Roa creep,
　　When moaning winds rend back her vapourous veil;
Wild Orinoco wedge-like split the deep,
　　　　Raging forth passion-pale;

Or a blue berg at sunrise glittering tall,
    Great as a town adrift come shining on
With sharp spires, gemlike as the mystical
        Clear city of Saint John.

Still the old tale; but they are children yet;
    O let their mothers have them while they may!
Soon it shall work, the strange mysterious fret
        That mars both toil and play.

The sea will claim its own; and some shall mourn;
    They also, they, but yet will surely go;
So surely as the planet to its bourne,
        The chamois to his snow.

'Father, dear father, bid us now God-speed;
    We cannot choose but sail, it thus befell.'
'Mother, dear mother —' 'Nay, 't is all decreed.
        Dear hearts, farewell, farewell!'

DORA.

A WAXING moon that, crescent yet,
    In all its silver beauty set,
And rose no more in the lonesome night
To shed full-orbed its longed-for light.

Then was it dark ; on wold and lea,
 In home, in heart, the hours were drear.
Father and mother could no light see,
 And the hearts trembled and there was fear.
— So on the mount, Christ's chosen three,
Unware that glory it did shroud,
Feared when they entered into the cloud.

She was the best part of love's fair
Adornment, life's God-given care,
As if He bade them guard His own,
Who should be soon anear His throne.
Dutiful, happy, and who say
When childhood smiles itself away,
' More fair than morn shall prove the day.'
Sweet souls so nigh to God that rest,
How shall be bettering of your best !
That promise heaven alone shall view,
That hope can ne'er with us come true,
That prophecy life hath not skill,
No, nor time leave that it fulfil.

There is but heaven, for childhood never
Can yield the all it meant, for ever.
Or is there earth, must wane to less
What dawned so close by perfectness.

How guileless, sweet, by gift divine,
How beautiful, dear child, was thine —

Spared all their grief of thee bereaven.
Winner, who had not greatly striven,
Hurts of sin shall not thee soil,
Carking care thy beauty spoil,
So early blest, so young forgiven.

Among the meadows fresh to view,
And in the woodland ways she grew,
On either side a hand to hold,
Nor the world's worst of evil knew,
Nor rued its miseries manifold,
Nor made discovery of its cold.
What more, like one with morn content,
Or of the morrow diffident,
Unconscious, beautiful she stood,
Calm, in young stainless maidenhood.
Then, with the last steps childhood trod,
Took up her fifteen years to God.

Farewell, sweet hope, not long to last,
All life is better for thy past.
Farewell till love with sorrow meet,
To learn that tears are obsolete.

SPERANZA.

Her younger sister, that Speranza hight.

ENGLAND puts on her purple, and pale, pale
　　With too much light, the primrose doth but wait
To meet the hyacinth ; then bower and dale
　　Shall lose her and each fairy woodland mate.
April forgets them, for their utmost sum
Of gift was silent, and the birds are come.

The world is stirring, many voices blend,
　　The English are at work in field and way :
All the good finches on their wives attend,
　　And emmets their new towns lay out in clay ;
Only the cuckoo-bird only doth say
Her beautiful name, and float at large all day.

Everywhere ring sweet clamours, chirrupping,
　　Chirping, that comes before the grasshopper :
The wide woods, flurried with the pulse of spring,
　　Shake out their wrinkled buds with tremor and stir ;
Small noises, little cries, the ear receives
Light as a rustling foot on last year's leaves.

All in deep dew the satisfied deep grass
    Looking straight upward stars itself with white,
Like ships in heaven full-sailed do long clouds pass
    Slowly o'er this great peace, and wide sweet light,
While through moist meads draws down yon rushy mere
Influent waters, sobbing, shining, clear.

Almost is rapture poignant; somewhat ails
    The heart and mocks the morning ; somewhat sighs,
And those sweet foreigners, the nightingales,
    Made restless with their love, pay down its price,
Even the pain ; then all the story unfold
Over and over again — yet 't is not told.

The mystery of the world whose name is life
    (One of the names of God) all-conquering wends
And works for aye with rest and cold at strife.
    Its pedigree goes up to Him and ends.
For it the lucent heavens are clear o'erhead,
And all the meads are made its natal bed.

Dear is the light, and eye-sight ever sweet,
    What see they all fair lower things that nurse,
No wonder, and no doubt ? Truly their meat,
Their kind, their field, their foes ; man's eyes are more ;
    Sight is man's having of the universe,
His pass to the majestical far shore.

But it is not enough, ah! not enough
   To look upon it and be held away,
And to be sure that, while we tread the rough,
   Remote, dull paths of this dull world, no ray
Shall pierce to us from the inner soul of things,
Nor voice thrill out from its deep master-strings.

'To show the skies, and tether to the sod!
   A daunting gift!' we mourn in our long strife,
And God is more than all our thought of God;
   E'en life itself more than our thought of life,
And that is all we know — and it is noon,
Our little day will soon be done — how soon!

O let us to ourselves be dutiful:
   We are not satisfied, we have wanted all,
Not alone beauty, but that Beautiful;
   A lifted veil, an answering mystical.
Ever men plead, and plain, admire, implore,
'Why gavest Thou so much — and yet — not more?

We are but let to look, and Hope is weighed.'
   Yet, say the Indian words of sweet renown,
'The doomèd tree withholdeth not her shade
   From him that bears the axe to cut her down;'
Is hope cut down, dead, doomèd, all is vain:
The third day dawns, she too has risen again

(For Faith is ours by gift, but Hope by right),
   And walks among us whispering as of yore :
'Glory and grace are thrown thee with the light ;
   Search, if not yet thou touch the mystic shore ;
Immanent beauty and good are nigh at hand,
For infants laugh and snowdrops bloom in the land.

Thou shalt have more anon.'   What more ? in sooth,
   The mother of to-morrow is to-day,
And brings forth after her kind.   There is no ruth
   On the heart's sigh, that 'more' is hidden away,
And man's to-morrow yet shall pine and yearn ;
He shall surmise, and he shall not discern,

But list the lark, and want the rapturous cries
   And passioning of morning stars that sing
Together ; mark the meadow-orchis rise
   And think it freckled after an angel's wing ;
Absent desire his land, and feel this, one
With the great drawing of the central sun.

But not to all such dower, for there be eyes
   Are colour-blind, and souls are spirit-blind.
Those never saw the blush in sunset skies,
Nor the others caught a sense not made of words
   As if were spirits about, that sailed the wind
And sank and settled on the boughs like birds.

Yet such for aye divided from us are
    As other galaxies that seem no more
Than a little golden millet-seed afar.
    Divided; swarming down some flat lee shore,
Then risen, while all the air that takes no word
Tingles, and trembles as with cries not heard.

For they can come no nearer. There is found
    No meeting point. We have pierced the lodging-place
Of stars that cluster'd with their peers lie bound,
    Embedded thick, sunk in the seas of space,
Fortunate orbs that know not night, for all
Are suns; — but we have never heard that call,

Nor learned it in our world, our citadel
    With outworks of a Power about it traced;
Nor why we needs must sin who would do well,
    Nor why the want of love, nor why its waste,
Nor how by dying of One should all be sped,
Nor where, O Lord, thou hast laid up our dead.

But Hope is ours by right, and Faith by gift.
    Though Time be as a moon upon the wane,
Who walk with Faith far up the azure lift
    Oft hear her talk of lights to wax again.
'If man be lost,' she cries, 'in this vast sea
Of being, — lost — he would be lost with Thee

Who for his sake once, as he hears, lost all.
For Thou wilt find him at the end of the days :
Then shall the flocking souls that thicker fall
    Than snowflakes on the everlasting ways
Be counted, gathered, claimed. — Will it be long ?
Earth has begun already her swan-song.

Who, even that might, would dwell for ever pent
    In this fair frame that doth the spirit inhearse,
Nor at the last grow weary and content,
    Die, and break forth into the universe,
And yet man would not all things — all — were new.'
Then saith the other, that one robed in blue :

'What if with subtle change God touch their eyes
    When he awakes them, — not far off, but here
In a new earth, this : not in any wise
    Strange, but more homely sweet, more heavenly dear,
Or if He roll away, as clouds disperse
Somewhat, and lo, that other universe.

O how 't were sweet new waked in some good hour,
    Long time to sit on a hillside green and high
There like a honeybee domed in a flower
    To feed unneath the azure bell o' the sky,
Feed in the midmost home and fount of light
Sown thick with stars at noonday as by night

To watch the flying faultless ones wheel down,
   Alight, and run along some ridgèd peak,
Their feet adust from orbs of old renown,
   Procyon or Mazzaroth, haply; — when they speak
Other-world errands wondrous, all discern
That would be strange, there would be much to learn.

Ay, and it would be sweet to share unblamed
   Love's shining truths that tell themselves in tears,
Or to confess and be no more ashamed
   The wrongs that none can right through earthly years;
And seldom laugh, because the tenderness
Calm, perfect, would be more than joy — would bless.

I tell you it were sweet to have enough,
   And be enough.   Among the souls forgiven
In presence of all worlds, without rebuff
   To move, and feel the excellent safety leaven
With peace that awe must loss and the grave survive —
But palpitating moons that are alive

Nor shining fogs swept up together afar,
   Vast as a thought of God, in the firmament;
No, and to dart as light from star to star
   Would not long time man's yearning soul content:
Albeit were no more ships and no more sea,
He would desire his new earth presently.

Leisure to learn it.   Peoples would be here;
 They would come on in troops, and take at will
The forms, the faces they did use to wear
 With life's first splendours — raiment rich with skill
Of broidery, carved adornments, crowns of gold ;
Still would be sweet to them the life of old.

Then might be gatherings under golden shade,
 Where dust of water drifts from some sheer fall,
Cooling day's ardour.   There be utterance made
 Of comforted love, dear freedom after thrall,
Large longings of the Seer, through earthly years
An everlasting burden, but no tears.

Egypt's adopted child might tell of lore
 They taught him underground in shrines all dim,
And of the live tame reptile gods that wore
 Gold anklets on their feet.   And after him,
With fairest eyes ere met of mortal ken,
Glorious, forgiven, might speak the mother of men.

Talk of her apples gather'd by the marge
 Of lapsing Gihon.   ' Thus one spoke, I stood,
I ate.'   Or next the mariner-saint enlarge
 Right quaintly on his ark of gopher wood
To wandering men through high grass meads that ran
Or sailed the sea Mediterranean.

It might be common — earth afforested
   Newly, to follow her great ones to the sun,
When from transcendent aisles of gloom they sped
   Some work august (there would be work) now done.
And list, and their high matters strive to scan
The seekers after God, and lovers of man,

Sitting together in amity on a hill,
   The Saint of Visions from Greek Patmos come —
Aurelius, lordly, calm-eyed, as of will
   Austere, yet having rue on lost, lost Rome,
And with them One who drank a fateful bowl,
And to the unknown God trusted his soul.

The mitred Cranmer pitied even there
   (But could it be?) for that false hand which signed
O, all pathetic — no.   But it might bear
   To soothe him marks of fire — and gladsome kind
The man, as all of joy him well beseemed
Who 'lighted on a certain place and dreamed.'

And fair with the meaning of life their divine brows,
   The daughters of well-doing famed in song;
But what! could old-world love for child, for spouse,
   For land, content through lapsing eons long?
Oh for a watchword strong to bridge the deep
And satisfy of fulness after sleep.

What know we ? Whispers fall, '*And the last first,*
   And the first last.' The child before the king ?
The slave before that man a master erst ?
   The woman before her lord ? Shall glory fling
The rolls aside — time raze out triumphs past ?
They sigh, ' *And the last first, and the first last.*'

Answers that other, ' Lady, sister, friend,
   It is enough, for I have worshipped Life;
With Him that is the Life man's life shall blend,
   E'en now the sacred heavens do help his strife,
There do they knead his bread and mix his cup,
And all the stars have leave to bear him up.

Yet must he sink and fall away to a sleep,
   As did his Lord. This Life his worshippèd
Religion, Life. The silence may be deep,
   Life listening, watching, waiting by His dead,
Till at the end of days they wake full fain
Because their King, the Life, doth love and reign.

I know the King shall come to that new earth,
   And His feet stand again as once they stood,
In His man's eyes will shine Time's end and worth
   The chiefest beauty and the chiefest good,
And all shall have the all and in it bide,
And every soul of man be satisfied.

THE BEGINNING.

'THEY tell strange things of the primeval earth,
    But things that be are never strange to those
Among them. And we know what it was like,
Many are sure they walked in it; the proof
This, the all gracious, all admirèd whole
Called life, called world, called thought, was all as one,
Nor yet divided more than that old earth
Among the tribes. Self was not fully come —
Self was asleep, embedded in the whole.

I too dwelt once in a primeval world,
Such as they tell of, all things wonderful;
Voices, ay visions, people grand and tall
Thronged in it, but their talk was overhead
And bore scant meaning, that one wanted not
Whose thought was sight as yet unbound of words,
This kingdom of heaven having entered through
Being a little child.
               Such as can see,
Why should they doubt? The childhood of a race,
The childhood of a soul, hath neither doubt
Nor fear. Where all is super-natural

The guileless heart doth feed on it, no more
Afraid than angels are of heaven.

      Who saith
Another life, the next one shall not have
Another childhood growing gently thus,
Able to bear the poignant sweetness, take
The rich long awful measure of its peace,
Endure the presence sublime.

       I saw
Once in that earth primeval, once — a face,
A little face that yet I dream upon.'

' Of this world was it ? '
      ' Not of this world — no,
In the beginning — for methinks it was
In the beginning but an if you ask
How long ago, time was not then, nor date
For marking.   It was always long ago,
E'en from the first recalling of it, long
And long ago.
    And I could walk, and went,
Led by the hand through a long mead at morn,
Bathed in a ravishing excess of light.
It throbbed, and as it were fresh fallen from heaven,
Sank deep into the meadow grass.   The sun
Gave every blade a bright and a dark side,
Glitter'd on buttercups that topped them, slipped
To soft red puffs, by some called holy-hay.

The wide oaks in their early green stood still
And took delight in it.   Brown specks that made
Very sweet noises quivered in the blue ;
Then they came down and ran along the brink
Of a long pool, and they were birds.

       The pool
Pranked at the edges with pale peppermint,
A rare amassment of veined cuckoo flowers
And flags blue-green was lying below.   This all
Was sight it condescended not to words
Till memory kissed the charmèd dream.

       The mead
Hollowing and heaving, in the hollows fair
With dropping roses fell away to it,
A strange sweet place ; upon its further side
Some people gently walking took their way
Up to a wood beyond ; and also bells
Sang, floated in the air, hummed — what you will.'

'Then it was Sunday ? '

       'Sunday was not yet ;
It was a holiday, for all the days
Were holy.   It was not our day of rest
(The earth for all her rolling asks not rest,
For she was never weary).

       It was sweet,
Full of dear leisure and perennial peace,
As very old days when life went easily,

Before mankind had lost the wise, the good
Habit of being happy.
    For the pool
A beauteous place it was as might be seen,
That led one down to other meads, and had
Clouds and another sky. I thought to go
Deep down in it, and walk that steep clear slope.

Then she who led me reached the brink, her foot
Staying to talk with one who met her there.
Here were fresh marvels, sailing things whose vans
Floated them on above the flowering flags.
We moved a little onward, paused again,
And here there was a break in these, and here
There came the vision; for I stooped to gaze
So far as my small height would let me — gaze
Into that pool to see the fishes dart,
And in a moment from her under hills
Came forth a little child who lived down there,
Looked up at me and smiled. We could not talk,
But looked and loved each other. I a hand
Held out to her, so she to me, but ah,
She would not come. Her home, her little bed,
Was doubtless under that soft shining thing
The water, and she wanted not to run
Among red sorrel spires, and fill her hand
In the dry warmèd grass with cowslip buds.

Awhile our feeding hearts all satisfied,
Took in the blue of one another's eyes,
Two dimpled creatures, rose-lipped innocent.
But when we fain had kissed — O ! the end came,
For snatched aloft, held in the nurse's arms,
She parting with her lover I was borne
Far from that little child.

      And no one knew
She lived down there, but only I ; and none
Sought for her, but I yearned for her and left
Part of myself behind, as the lambs leave
Their wool upon a thorn.'

       ' And was she seen
Never again, nor known for what she was ? '

' Never again, for we did leave anon
The pasture and the pool. I know not where
They lie, and sleep a heaven on earth, but know
From thenceforth yearnings for a lost delight ;
On certain days I dream about her still.'

'WHERE do you go, Bob, when you're fast asleep?'
    'Where? O well, once I went into a deep
Mine, father told of, and a cross man said
He'd make me help to dig, and eat black bread.
I saw the Queen once, in her room, quite near.
She said, "You rude boy, Bob, how came you here?"'

'Was it like mother's boudoir?'
                  'Grander far,
Gold chairs and things — all over diamonds — Ah!'

'You're sure it was the Queen?'
               'Of course, a crown
Was on her, and a spangly purple gown.'

'I went to heaven last night.'
            'O Lily, no,
How could you?'
            'Yes I did, they told me so,
And my best doll, my favourite, with the blue
Frock, Jasmine, I took her to heaven too.'

'What was it like?'

　　　　　　　　'A kind of — I can't tell —
A sort of orchard place in a long dell,
With trees all over flowers.　And there were birds
Who could do talking, say soft pretty words;
They let me stroke them, and I showed it all
To Jasmine.　And I heard a blue dove call,
"Child, this is heaven."　I was not frightened when
It spoke, I said " Where are the angels then? " '

'Well.'

　　　　　　'So it said, " Look up and you shall see."
There were two angels sitting in the tree,
As tall as mother; they had long gold hair.
They let drop down the fruit they gather'd there
And little angels came for it — so sweet.
Here they were beggar children in the street,
And the dove said they had the prettiest things,
And wore their best frocks every day.'

　　　　　　　　　　　'And wings,
Had they no wings?'

　　　　　　　　'O yes, and lined with white
Like swallow wings, so soft — so very light
Fluttering about.'

　　　　　'Well.'

　　　　　　　　'Well, I did not stay,
So that was all.'

　　　　　'They made you go away?'

The bell-bird is an Australian bird.

Evesham is a small town on the Avon, not far from Stratford-on-Avon. The vale of Evesham is celebrated for its fruit orchards, especially of plum-trees, and it is a lovely sight when they are in flower. The river is very beautiful there, and the market people and visitors often gather on the bridge and in the grassy church-yard at noon to hear the celebrated bells in the "bell tower" of the old abbey. Those bells are thought to have the finest peal in England. One who has often listened to them says, "I always think there is something almost too pure and ethereal for this world when I hear the sound of those bells floating down the river; and at night, when I have heard them ring out 'There's nae luck about the house,' the pathetic sweetness is almost unbearable; but most people like their 'Home, sweet home' best. It is such old-world things as they are that *make a home*, and tie the hearts that dwell about them to want their voices for ever."

'I did not go — but — I was gone.'

'I know.'

'But it's a pity, Bob, we never go
Together.'

'Yes, and have no dreams to tell,
But the next day both know it all quite well.'

'And, Bob, if I could dream you came with me
You would be there perhaps.'

'Perhaps — we'll see.'

———◦◦———

THE BELL-BIRD.

'TOLL —
　　　　Toll.'　'The bell-bird sounding far away,
　Hid in a myall grove.'　He raised his head,
The bush glowed scarlet in descending day,
　A masterless wild country — and he said,
My father ('Toll.')　'Full oft by her to stray,
　As if a spirit called, have I been led ;
Oft seems she as an echo in my soul
('Toll.') from my native towers by Avon (' Toll ').

('Toll.')　Oft as in a dream I see full fain
　The bell-tower beautiful that I love well,
A seemly cluster with her churches twain.

I hear adown the river faint and swell
And lift upon the air that sound again,
 It is, it is — how sweet no tongue can tell,
For all the world-wide breadth of shining foam,
The bells of Evesham chiming " Home, sweet home."

The mind hath mastery thus — it can defy
 The sense, and make all one as it DID HEAR —
Nay, I mean more ; the wraiths of sound gone by
 Rise ; they are present 'neath this dome all clear.
ONE, sounds the bird — a pause — then doth supply
 Some ghost of chimes the void expectant ear ;
Do they ring bells in heaven ? The learnedest soul
Shall not resolve me such a question. (' Toll.')

(' Toll.') Say I am a boy, and fishing stand
 By Avon (' Toll.') on line and rod intent,
How glitters deep in dew the meadow land —
 What, dost thou flit, thy ministry all spent,
Not many days we hail such visits bland,
 Why steal so soon the rare enravishment?
Ay gone ! the soft deceptive echoes roll
Away, and faint into remoteness.' (' Toll.')

While thus he spoke the doom'd sun touched his bed
 In scarlet, all the palpitating air
Still loyal waited on. He dipped his head,
 Then all was over, and the dark was there ;

And northward, lo! a star, one likewise red
   But lurid, starts from out her day-long lair,
Her fellows trail behind; she bears her part,
The balefullest star that shines, the Scorpion's heart

Or thus of old men feigned, and then did fear,
   Then straight crowd forth the great ones of the sky
In flashing flame at strife to reach more near.
   The little children of Infinity,
They next look down as to report them ' Here,'
   From deeps all thoughts despair and heights past high,
Speeding, not sped, no rest, no goal, no shore,
Still to rush on till time shall be no more.

' Loved vale of Evesham, 't is a long farewell,
   Not laden orchards nor their April snow
These eyes shall light upon again; the swell
   And whisper of thy storied river know,
Nor climb the hill where great old Montfort fell
   In a good cause hundreds of years ago ;
So fall'n, elect to live till life's ally,
The river of recorded deeds, runs dry.

This land is very well, this air,' saith he,
   ' Is very well, but we want echoes here.
Man's past to feed the air and move the sea ;
   Ages of toil make English furrows dear,

Enriched by blood shed for his liberty,
  Sacred by love's first sigh and life's last fear,
We come of a good nest, for it shall yearn
Poor birds of passage, but may not return,

Spread younger wings, and beat the winds afar.
  There sing more poets in that one small isle
Than all isles else can show — of such you are;
  Remote things come to you unsought erewhile,
Near things a long way round as by a star.
  Wild dreams!' He laughed, 'A sage right infantile;
With sacred fear behold life's waste deplored,
Undaunted by the leisure of the Lord.

Ay go, the island dream with eyes make good,
  Where Freedom rose, a lodestar to your race;
And Hope that leaning on her anchor stood
  Did smile it to her feet: a right small place.
Call her a mother, high such motherhood,
  Home in her name and duty in her face;
Call her a ship, her wide arms rake the clouds,
And every wind of God pipes in her shrouds.

Ay, all the more go you. But some have cried
  "The ship is breaking up;" they watch amazed
While urged toward the rocks by some that guide:
  Bad steering, reckless steering, she all dazed

Tempteth her doom; yet this have none denied
  Ships men have wrecked and palaces have razed,
But never was it known beneath the sun,
They of such wreckage built a goodlier one.

God help old England an't be thus, nor less
  God help the world.' Therewith my mother spake,
' Perhaps He will! by time, by faithlessness,
  By the world's want long in the dark awake,
I think He must be almost due : the stress
  Of the great tide of life, sharp misery's ache,
In a recluseness of the soul we rue
Far off, but yet — He must be almost due.

God manifest again, the coming King.'
  Then said my father, ' I beheld erewhile,
Sitting up dog-like to the sunrising,
  The giant doll in ruins by the Nile,
With hints of red that yet to it doth cling,
  Fell, battered, and bewigged its cheeks were vile,
A body of evil with its angel fled,
Whom and his fellow fiends men worshippèd.

The gods die not, long shrouded on their biers,
  Somewhere they live, and live in memory yet;
Were not the Israelites for forty years
  Hid from them in the desert to forget —

Did they forget? no more than their lost feres
    Sons of to-day with faces southward set,
Who dig for buried lore long ages fled,
And sift for it the sand and search the dead.

Brown Egypt gave not one great poet birth,
    But man was better than his gods, with lay
He soothed them restless, and they zoned the earth,
    And crossed the sea; there drank immortal praise;
Then from his own best self with glory and worth
    And beauty dowered he them for dateless days.
Ever " their sound goes forth " from shore to shore,
When was there known an hour that they lived more.

Because they are beloved and not believed,
    Admired not feared, they draw men to their feet;
All once, rejected, nothing now, received
    Where once found wanting, now the most complete;
Man knows to-day, though manhood stand achieved,
    His cradle-rockers made a rustling sweet;
That king reigns longest which did lose his crown,
Stars that by poets shine are stars gone down.

Still drawn obedient to an unseen hand,
    From purer heights comes down the yearning west,
Like to that eagle in the morning land,
    That swooping on her predatory quest,

Did from the altar steal a smouldering brand,
   The which she bearing home it burned her nest,
And her wide pinions of their plumes bereaven,
Spoiled for glad spiring up the steeps of heaven.

I say the gods live, and that reign abhor,
   And will the nations it should dawn ? Will they
Who ride upon the perilous edge of war ?
   Will such as delve for gold in this our day ?
Neither the world will, nor the age will, nor
   The soul — and what, it cometh now ? Nay, nay,
The weighty sphere, unready for release,
Rolls far in front of that o'ermastering peace.

Wait and desire it ; life waits not, free there
   To good, to evil, thy right perilous —
All shall be fair, and yet it is not fair.
   I thank my God He takes th' advantage thus ;
He doth not greatly hide, but still declare
   Which side He is on and which He loves, to us,
While life impartial aid to both doth lend,
And heed not which the choice nor what the end.

Among the few upright, O to be found,
   And ever search the nobler path, my son,
Nor say 't is sweet to find me common ground
   Too high, too good, shall leave the hours alone —

Nay, though but one stood on the height renowned,
  Deny not hope or will, to be that one.
Is it the many fall'n shall lift the land,
The race, the age!— Nay, 't is the few that stand.'

While in the lamplight hearkening I sat mute,
  Methought ' How soon this fire must needs burn out '
Among the passion flowers and passion fruit
  That from the wide verandah hung, misdoubt
Was mine.   ' And wherefore made I thus long suit
  To leave this old white head ?   His words devout,
His blessing not to hear who loves me so —
He that is old, right old — I will not go.'

But ere the dawn their counsels wrought with me,
  And I went forth ; alas that I so went
Under the great gum-forest canopy,
  The light on every silken filament
Of every flower, a quivering ecstasy
  Of perfect paleness made it ; sunbeams sent
Up to the leaves with sword-like flash endued
Each turn of that grey drooping multitude.

I sought to look as in the light of one
  Returned.   ' Will this be strange to me that day ?
Flocks of green parrots clamorous in the sun
  Tearing out milky maize — stiff cacti grey

As old men's beards — here stony ranges lone,
  Their dust of mighty flocks upon their way
To water, cloudlike on the bush afar,
Like smoke that hangs where old-world cities are.

Is it not made man's last endowment here
  To find a beauty in the wilderness ;
Feel the lorn moor above his pastures dear,
  Mountains that may not house and will not bless
To draw him even to death ?   He must insphere
  His spirit in the open, so doth less
Desire his feres, and more that unvex'd wold
And fine afforested hills, his dower of old.

But shall we lose again that new-found sense
  Which sees the earth less for our tillage fair ?
Oh, let her speak with her best eloquence
  To me, but not her first and her right rare
Can equal what I may not take from hence.
  The gems are left : it is not otherwhere
The wild Nepèan cleaves her matchless way,
Nor Sydney harbour shall outdo the day.

Adding to day this — that she lighteth it.'
  But I beheld again, and as must be
With a world-record by a spirit writ,
  It was more beautiful than memory,
                7

Than hope was more complete.

        Tall brigs did sit
 Each in her berth the pure flood placidly,
Their topsails drooping 'neath the vast blue dome
Listless, as waiting to be sheeted home.

And the great ships with pulse-like throbbing clear,
 Majestical of mien did take their way
Like living creatures from some grander sphere,
 That having boarded ours thought good to stay,
Albeit enslaved. They most divided here
 From God's great art and all his works in clay,
In that their beauty lacks, though fair it shows
That divine waste of beauty only He bestows.

The day was young, scarce out the harbour lights
 That morn I sailed: low sun-rays tremulous
On golden loops sped outward. Yachts in flights
 Flutter'd the water air-like clear, while thus
It crept for shade among brown rocky bights
 With cassia crowned and palms diaphanous,
And boughs ripe fruitage dropping fitfully,
That on the shining ebb went out to sea.

' Home,' saith the man self-banishèd, ' my son
 Shall now go home.' Therewith he sendeth him
Abroad, and knows it not, but thence is won,
 Rescued, the son's true home. His mind doth limn

Beautiful pictures of it, there is none
   So dear, a new thought shines erewhile but dim,
'That was my home, a land past all compare,
Life, and the poetry of life, are there.'

But no such thought drew near to me that day ;
   All the new worlds flock forth to greet the old,
All the young souls bow down to own its sway,
   Enamoured of strange richness manifold ;
Not to be stored, albeit they seek for aye,
   Besieging it for its own life to hold,
E'en as Al Mamoun fain for treasures hid,
Stormed with an host th' inviolate pyramid.

And went back foiled but wise to walled Bagdad.
   So I, so all. The treasure sought not found,
But some divine tears found to superadd
   Themselves to a long story. The great round
Of yesterdays, their pathos sweet as sad,
   Found to be only as to-day, close bound
With us, we hope some good thing yet to know,
But God is not in haste, while the lambs grow

The Shepherd leadeth softly. It is great
   The journey, and the flock forgets at last
(Earth ever working to obliterate
   The landmarks) when it halted, where it passed

And words confuse, and time doth ruinate,
   And memory fail to hold a theme so vast;
There is request for light, but the flock feeds,
And slowly ever on the Shepherd leads.

'Home,' quoth my father, and a glassy sea
   Made for the stars a mirror of its breast,
While southing, pennon-like, in bravery
   Of long drawn gold they trembled to their rest.
Strange the first night and morn, when Destiny
   Spread out to float on, all the mind oppressed;
Strange on their outer roof to speed forth thus,
And know th' uncouth sea-beasts stared up at us.

But yet more strange the nights of falling rain,
   That splashed without — a sea-coal fire within;
Life's old things gone astern, the mind's disdain,
   For murmurous London makes soft rhythmic din.
All courtier thoughts that wait on words would fain
   Express that sound. The words are not to win
Till poet made, but mighty, yet so mild
Shall be as cooing of a cradle-child.

Sensation like a piercing arrow flies,
   Daily out-going thought. This Adamhood,
This weltering river of mankind that hies
   Adown the street; it cannot be withstood.

The richest mundane miles not otherwise
  Than by a symbol keep possession good,
Mere symbol of division, and they hold
The clear pane sacred, the unminted gold

And wild outpouring of all wealth not less.
  Why this? A million strong the multitude,
And safe, far safer than our wilderness
  The walls; for them it daunts with right at feud,
Itself declares for law; yet sore the stress
  On steeps of life: what power to ban and bless,
Saintly denial, waste inglorious,
Desperate want, and riches fabulous.

Of souls what beautiful embodiment
  For some; for some what homely housing writ;
What keen-eyed men who beggared of content
  Eat bread well earned as they had stolen it;
What flutterers after joy that forward went,
  And left them in the rear unqueened, unfit
For joy, with light that faints in strugglings drear
Of all things good the most awanting here.

Some in the welter of this surging tide
  Move like the mystic lamps, the Spirits Seven,
Their burning love runs kindling far and wide,
  That fire they needed not to steal from heaven,

'T was a free gift flung down with them to bide,
   And be a comfort for the hearts bereaven,
A warmth, a glow, to make the failing store
And parsimony of emotion more.

What glorious dreams in that find harbourage,
   The phantom of a crime stalks this beside,
And those might well have writ on some past page,
   In such an hour, of such a year, we — died,
Put out our souls, took the mean way, false wage,
   Course cowardly ; and if we be denied
The life once loved, we cannot alway rue
The loss ; let be : what vails so sore ado.

And faces pass of such as give consent
   To live because 't is not worth while to die ;
This never knew the awful tremblement
   When some great fear sprang forward suddenly,
Its other name being hope — and there forthwent
   As both confronted him a rueful cry
From the heart's core, one urging him to dare,
'Now ! now ! Leap now.' The other, 'Stand, forbear.'

A nation reared in brick. How shall this be ?
   Nor by excess of life death overtake.
To die in brick of brick her destiny,
   And as the hamadryad eats the snake

His wife, and then the snake his son, so she
    Air not enough, ' though everyone doth take
A little,' water scant, a plague of gold,
Light out of date — a multitude born old.

And then a three-day siege might be the end ;
    E'en now the rays get muddied struggling down
Through heaven's vasty lofts, and still extend
    The miles of brick and none forbid, and none
Forbode ; a great world-wonder that doth send
    High fame abroad, and fear no setting sun,
But helpless she through wealth that flouts the day
And through her little children, even as they.

But forth of London, and all visions dear
    To eastern poets of a watered land
Are made the commonplace of nature here,
    Sweet rivers always full, and always bland.
Beautiful, beautiful !   What runlets clear
    Twinkle among the grass.   On every hand
Fall in the common talk from lips around
The old names of old towns and famous ground.

It is not likeness only charms the sense,
    Not difference only sets the mind aglow,
It is the likeness in the difference,
    Familiar language spoken on the snow,

To have the Perfect in the Present tense,
　　To hear the ploughboy whistling, and to know,
It smacks of the wild bush, that tune — 'T is ours,
And look ! the bank is pale with primrose flowers,

What veils of tender mist make soft the lea,
　　What bloom of air the height ; no veils confer
On warring thought or softness or degree
　　Or rest.　Still falling, conquering, strife and stir.
For this religion pays indemnity.
　　She pays her enemies for conquering her,
And then her friends ; while ever, and in vain
Lots for a seamless coat are cast again

Whose it shall be ; unless it shall endow
　　Thousands of thousands it can fall to none,
But faith and hope are not so simple now,
　　As in the year of our redemption — One.
The pencil of pure light must disallow
　　Its name and scattering, many hues put on,
And faith and hope low in the valley feel,
There it is well with them, 't is very well.

The land is full of vision, voices call.
　　Can spirits cast a shadow ?　Ay, I trow
Past is not done, and over is not all,
　　Opinion dies to live and wanes to grow,

The gossamer of thought doth filmlike fall,
  On fallows after dawn make shimmering show,
And with old arrow-heads, her earliest prize,
Mix learning's latest guess and last surmise.

There heard I pipes of fame, saw wrens 'about
  That time when kings go forth to battle' dart,
Full valorous atoms pierced with song, and stout
  To dare, and down yclad; I shared the smart
Of grievèd cushats, bloom of love, devout
  Beyond man's thought of it. Old song my heart
Rejoiced, but O mine own forelders' ways
To look on, and their fashions of past days.

The ponderous craft of arms I craved to see,
  Knights, burghers, filtering through those gates ajar,
Their age of serfdom with my spirit free;
  We cannot all have wisdom; some there are
Believe a star doth rule their destiny,
  And yet they think to overreach the star,
For thought can weld together things apart,
And contraries find meeting in the heart.

In the deep dust at Suez without sound
  I saw the Arab children walk at eve,
Their dark untroubled eyes upon the ground,
  A part of Time's grave quiet. I receive

Since then a sense, as nature might have found
　Love kin to man's that with the past doth grieve;
And lets on waste and dust of ages fall
Her tender silences that mean it all.

We have it of her, with her; it were ill
　For men, if thought were widowed of the world,
Or the world beggared of her sons, for still
　A crownèd sphere with many gems impearled
She rolls because of them.　We lend her will
　And she yields love.　The past shall not be hurled
In the abhorrèd limbo while the twain,
Mother and son, hold partnership and reign.

She hangs out omens, and doth burdens dree.
　Is she in league with heaven?　That knows but One.
For man is not, and yet his work we see
　Full of unconscious omen darkly done.
I saw the ring-stone wrought at Avebury
　To frame the face of the midwinter sun,
Good luck that hour they thought from him forth smiled
At midwinter the Sun did rise — the Child.

Still would the world divine though man forbore,
　And what is beauty but an omen? — what
But life's deep divination cast before,
　Omen of coming love?　Hard were man's lot,

With love and toil together at his door,
  But all-convincing eyes hath beauty got;
His love is beautiful, and he shall sue.
Toil for her sake is sweet, the omen true.

Love, love, and come it must, then life is found
  Beforehand that was whole and fronting care,
A torn and broken half in durance bound
  That mourns and makes request for its right fair
Remainder, with forlorn eyes cast around
  To search for what is lost, that unaware
With not an hour's forebodement makes the day
From henceforth less or more for ever and aye.

Her name — my love's — I knew it not; who says
  Of vagrant doubt for such a cause that stirs
His fancy shall not pay arrearages
  To all sweet names that might perhaps be hers?
The doubts of love are powers. His heart obeys,
  The world is in them, still to love defers,
Will play with him for love, but when 't begins
The play is high, and the world always wins.

For 't is the maiden's world, and his no more.
  Now thus it was: with new found kin flew by
The temperate summer; every wheatfield wore
  Its gold, from house to house in ardency

Of heart for what they showed I westward bore —
   My mother's land, her native hills drew nigh;
I was — how green, how good old earth can be —
Beholden to that land for teaching me.

And parted from my fellows, and went on
   To feel the spiritual sadness spread
Adown long pastoral hollows.   And anon
   Did words recur in far remoteness said:
'See the deep vale ere dews are dried and gone,
   Where my so happy life in peace I led,
And the great shadow of the Beacon lies —
See little Ledbury trending up the rise.

With peakèd houses and high market hall —
   An oak each pillar — reared in the old days.
And here was little Ledbury, quaint withal,
   The forest felled, her lair and sheltering place
She long time left in age pathetical.
   ' Great oaks ' methought, as I drew near to gaze,
' Were but of small account when these came down,
Drawn rough-hewn in to serve the tree-girt town.

And thus and thus of it will question be
   The other side the world.'   I paused awhile
To mark.   ' The old hall standeth utterly
   Without or floor or side, a comely pile,

A house on pillars, and by destiny
   Drawn under its deep roof I saw a file
Of children slowly through their way make good,
And lifted up mine eyes — and there — SHE STOOD.

She was so stately that her youthful grace
   Drew out, it seemed, my soul unto the air,
Astonished out of breathing by her face
   So fain to nest itself in nut-brown hair
Lying loose about her throat. But that old place
   Proved sacred, she just fully grown too fair
For such a thought. The dimples that she had!
She was so truly sweet that it was sad.

I was all hers. That moment gave her power —
   And whom, nay what she was, I scarce might know,
But felt I had been born for that good hour.
   The perfect creature did not move, but so
As if ordained to claim all grace for dower.
   She leaned against the pillar, and below
Three almost babes, her care, she watched the while
With downcast lashes and a musing smile.

I had been 'ware without a rustic treat,
   Waggons bedecked with greenery stood anigh,
A swarm of children in the cheerful street
   With girls to marshal them; but all went by

And none I noted save this only sweet:
    Too young her charge more venturous sport to try,
With whirling baubles still they play content,
And softly rose their lisping babblement.

'O what a pause! to be so near, to mark
    The locket rise and sink upon her breast;
The shadow of the lashes lieth dark
    Upon her cheek. O fleeting time, O rest!
A slant ray finds the gold, and with a spark
    And flash it answers, now shall be the best.
Her eyes she raises, sets their light on mine,
They do not flash nor sparkle — no — but shine.'

As I for very hopelessness made bold
    Did off my hat ere time there was for thought,
She with a gracious sweetness, calm, not cold,
    Acknowledged me, but brought my chance to nought.
'This vale of imperfection doth not hold
    A lovelier bud among its loveliest wrought!
She turns,' methought 'O do not quite forget
To me remains for ever — that we met.'

And straightway I went forth, I could no less,
    Another light unwot of fall'n on me,
And rare elation and high happiness
    Some mighty power set hands of mastery

Among my heartstrings, and they did confess
 With wild throbs inly sweet, that minstrelsy
A nightingale might dream so rich a strain,
And pine to change her song for sleep again.

The harp thrilled ever: O with what a round
 And series of rich pangs fled forth each note
Oracular, that I had found, had found
 (Head waters of old Nile held less remote)
Golden Dorado, dearest, most renowned;
 But when as 't were a sigh did overfloat,
Shaping 'how long, not long shall this endure,
Au jour le jour' methought, '*Au jour le jour.*'

The minutes of that hour my heart knew well
 Were like the fabled pint of golden grain,
Each to be counted, paid for, till one fell,
 Grew, shot up to another world amain,
And he who dropped might climb it, there to dwell.
 I too, I clomb another world full fain,
But was she there? O what would be the end,
Might she nor there appear, nor I descend?

All graceful as a palm the maiden stood;
 Men say the palm of palms in tropic Isles
Doth languish in her deep primeval wood,
 And want the voice of man, his home, his smiles,

Nor flourish but in his dear neighborhood;
　　She too shall want a voice that reconciles,
A smile that charms — how sweet would heaven so
　　　　please —
To plant her at my door over far seas.

I paced without, nor ever liege in truth
　　His sovran lady watched with more grave eyes
Of reverence, and she nothing ware forsooth,
　　Did standing charm the soul with new surprise.
Moving flow on a dimpled dream of youth.
　　Look! look! a sunbeam on her.　Ay, but lies
The shade more sweetly now she passeth through
To join her fellow maids returned anew.

I saw (myself to bide unmarked intent)
　　Their youthful ease and pretty airs sedate,
They are so good, they are so innocent,
　　Those Islanders, they learn their part so late,
Of life's demand right careless, dwell content
　　Till the first love's first kiss shall consecrate
Their future to a world that can but be
By their sweet martyrdom and ministry.

Most happy of God's creatures.　Afterward
　　More than all women married thou wilt be,
E'en to the soul.　One glance desired afford,
　　More than knight's service might'st thou ask of me.

Not any chance is mine, not the best word,
  No, nor the salt of life withouten thee.
Must this all end, is my day so soon o'er?
Untroubled violet eyes, look once, — once more.

No, not a glance: the low sun lay and burned,
  Now din of drum and cry of fife withal,
Blithe teachers mustering frolic swarms returned,
  And new-world ways in that old market hall,
Sweet girls, fair women, how my whole heart yearned
  Her to draw near who made my festival.
With others closing round, time speeding on,
How soon she would be gone, she would be gone!

Ay, but I thought to track the rustic wains,
  Their goal desired to note, but not anigh,
They creaking down long hop yerested lanes
  'Neath the abiding flush of that north sky.
I ran, my horse I fetched, but fate ordains
  Love shall breed laughter when th' unloving spy.
As I drew rein to watch the gathered crowd,
With sudden mirth an old wife laughed aloud.

Her cheeks like winter apples red of hue,
  ' Her glance aside. To whom her speech — to me?
' I know the thing you go about to do —
  The lady —' ' What! the lady —' 'Sir,' saith she,

8

('I thank you kindly, sir), I tell you true
    She's gone,' and 'here's a coil' methought 'will be.'
'Gone — where?'   ''T is past my wit forsooth to say
If they went Malvern way or Hereford way.

A carriage took her up — where three roads meet
    They needs must pass; you may o'ertake it yet.'
And 'Oyez, Oyez' peals adown the street,
    'Lost, lost, a golden heart with pearls beset.'
'I know her, sir? — not I.   To help this treat,
    Many strange ladies from the country met.'
'O heart beset with pearls! my hope was crost.
Farewell, good dame.   Lost! oh my lady lost.'

And 'Oyez, Oyez' following after me
    On my great errand to the sundown went.
Lost, lost, and lost, whenas the cross road flee
    Up tumbled hills, on each for eyes attent
A carriage creepeth.
                      'Though in neither she,
    I ne'er shall know life's worst impoverishment,
An empty heart.   No time, I stake my all,
To right! and chase the rose-red evenfall.

Fly up, good steed, fly on.   Take the sharp rise
    As 't were a plain.   A lady sits; but one.
So fast the pace she turns in startled wise,
    She sets her gaze on mine and all is done.

" Persian Roxana " might have raised such eyes
    When Alexander sought her.   Now the sun
Dips, and my day is over; turn and fleet
The world fast flies, again do three roads meet.'

I took the left, and for some cause unknown
    Full fraught of hope and joy the way pursued,
Yet chose strong reasons speeding up alone
    To fortify me 'gainst a shock more rude.
E'en so the diver carrieth down a stone
    In hand, lest he float up before he would,
And end his walk upon the rich sea-floor,
Those pearls he failed to grasp never to look on more.

Then as the low moon heaveth, waxen white,
    The carriage, and it turns into a gate.
Within sit three in pale pathetic light.
    O surely one of these my love, my fate.
But ere I pass they wind away from sight.
    Then cottage casements glimmer.   All elate
I cross a green, there yawns with opened latch
A village hostel capped in comely thatch.

'The same world made for all is made for each.
    To match a heart's magnificence of hope,
How shall good reason best high action teach
    To win of custom, and with home to cope

How warrantably may he hope to win
    A star, that wants it?   Shall he lie and grope,
No, truly. — I will see her; tell my tale,
See her this once, — and if I fail — I fail.'

Thus with myself I spoke.   A rough brick floor
    Made the place homely ; I would rest me there.
But how to sleep?   Forth of the unlocked door
    I passed at midnight, lustreless white air
Made strange the hour, that ecstasy not o'er
    I moved among the shadows, all my care —
Counted a shadow — her drawn near to bless,
Impassioned out of fear, rapt, motionless.

Now a long pool and water-hens at rest
    (As doughty seafolk dusk, at Malabar)
A few pale stars lie trembling on its breast.
    Hath the Most High of all His host afar
One most supremely beautiful, one best,
    Dearest of all the flock, one favourite star?
His Image given, in part the children know
They love one first and best.   It may be so.

Now a long hedge ; here dream the woolly folk ;
    A majesty of silence is about.
Transparent mist rolls off the pool like smoke,
    And Time is in his trance and night devout.

Now the still house.   O an I knew she woke
  I could not look, the sacred moon sheds out
So many blessings on her rooftree low,
Each more pathetic that she nought doth know

I would not love a little, nor my start
  Make with the multitude that love and cease.
He gives too much that giveth half a heart,
  Too much for liberty, too much for peace.
Let me the first and best and highest impart,
  The whole of it, and heaven the whole increase!
For *that* were not too much.

                              (In the moon's wake
How the grass glitters, for her sweetest sake.)

I would toward her walk the silver floors.
  Love loathes an average — all extreme things deal
To love — sea-deep and dazzling height for stores.
  There are on Fortune's errant foot can steal,
Can guide her blindfold in at their own doors,
  Or dance elate upon her slippery wheel.
Courage! there are 'gainst hope can still advance,
Dowered with a sane, a wise extravagance.

A song
          To one a dreaming : when the dew
Falls, 't is a time for rest ; and when the bird
  Calls, 't is a time to wake, to wake for you.

A long-waking, aye, waking till a word
  Come from her coral mouth to be the true
Sum of all good heart wanted, ear hath heard.

    Yet if alas! might love thy dolour be,
Dream, dear heart dear, and do not dream of me.

I sing
         To one awakened, when the heart
  Cries 't is a day for thought, and when the soul
Sighs choose thy part, O choose thy part, thy part.
    I bring to one belovèd, bring my whole
Store, make in loving, make O make mine art
    More. Yet I ask no, ask no wishèd goal

But this — if loving might thy dolour be,
Wake, O my lady loved, and love not me.

'That which the many win, love's niggard sum,
  I will not, if love's all be left behind.
That which I am I cannot unbecome,
  My past not unpossess, nor future blind.
Let me all risk, and leave the deep heart dumb
  For ever, if that maiden sits enshrined
The saint of one more happy. She is she.
There is none other. Give her then to me.

Or else to be the better for her face
   Beholding it no more.'   Then all night through
The shadow moves with infinite dark grace.
   The light is on her windows, and the dew
Comforts the world and me, till in my place
   At moonsetting, when stars flash out to view,
Comes 'neath the cedar boughs a great repose,
The peace of one renouncing, and then a doze.

There was no dream, yet waxed a sense in me
   Asleep that patience was the better way,
Appeasement for a want that needs must be,
   Grew as the dominant mind forbore its sway,
Till whistling sweet stirred in the cedar tree —
   I started — woke — it was the dawn of day.
That was the end.   'Slow solemn growth of light,
Come what come will, remains to me this night.'

It was the end, with dew ordained to melt,
   How easily was learned, how all too soon
Not there, not thereabout such maiden dwelt.
   What was it promised me so fair a boon ?
Heart-hope is not less vain because heart-felt,
   Gone forth once more in search of her at noon
Through the sweet country side on hill, on plain,
I sought and sought many long days in vain.

To Malvern next, with feathery woodland hung,
   Whereto old Piers the Plowman came to teach,
On her green vasty hills the lay was sung,
   He too, it may be, lisping in his speech,
'To make the English sweet upon his tongue.'
   How many maidens beautiful, and each
Might him delight, that loved no other fair;
But Malvern blessed not me, — she was not there.

Then to that town, but still my fate the same.
   Crowned with old works that her right well beseem,
To gaze upon her field of ancient fame
   And muse on the sad thrall's most piteous dream,
By whom a ' shadow like an angel came,'
   Crying out on Clarence, its wild eyes agleam,
Accusing echoes here still falter and flee,
' That stabbed me on the field by Tewkesbury.'

It nothing 'vailed that yet I sought and sought,
   Part of my very self was left behind,
Till risen in wrath against th' o'ermastering thought,
   'Let me be thankful,' quoth the better mind,
Thankful for her, though utterly to nought
   She brings my heart's cry, and I live to find
A new self of the old self exigent
In the light of my divining discontent.

The picture of a maiden bidding 'Arise,
　　I am the Art of God. He shows by me
His great idea, so well as sin-stained eyes
　　Love aidant can behold it.'
　　　　　　　　　　　　　　Is this she?
Or is it mine own love for her supplies
　　The meaning and the power? Howe'er this be,
She is the interpreter by whom most near
Man's soul is drawn to beauty and pureness here.

The sweet idea, invisible hitherto,
　　Is in her face, unconscious delegate ;
That thing she wots not of ordained to do :
　　But also it shall be her votary's fate,
Through her his early days of ease to eschew,
　　Struggle with life and prove its weary weight.
All the great storms that rising rend the soul,
Are life in little, imaging the whole.

Ay, so as life is, love is, in their ken
　　Stars, infant yet, both thought to grasp, to keep,
Then came the morn of passionate splendour, when
　　So sweet the light, none but for bliss could weep,
And then the strife, the toil ; but we are men,
　　Strong, brave to battle with the stormy deep ;
Then fear — and then renunciation — then
Appeals unto the Infinite Pity — and sleep.

But after life the sleep is long. Not so
　With love. Love buried lieth not straight, not still,
Love starts, and after lull awakes to know
　All the deep things again. And next his will,
That dearest pang is, never to forego.
　He would all service, hardship, fret fulfill.
Unhappy love! and I of that great host
Unhappy love who cry, unhappy most.

Because renunciation was so short,
　The starvèd heart so easily awaked;
A dream could do it, a bud, a bird, a thought,
　But I betook me with that want which ached
To neighbour lands where strangeness with me wrought.
　The old work was so hale, its fitness slaked
Soul-thirst for truth. 'I knew not doubt nor fear,'
Its language, 'war or worship, sure sincere.'

Then where by Art the high did best translate
　Life's infinite pathos to the soul, set down
Beauty and mystery, that imperious hate
　On its best braveness doth and sainthood frown,
Nay more the MASTER's manifest pity — 'wait,
　Behold the palmgrove and the promised crown.
He suffers with thee, for thee. — Lo the Child!
Comfort thy heart; he certainly so smiled.'

Thus love and I wore through the winter time.
  Then saw her demon blush Vesuvius try,
Then evil ghosts white from the awful prime,
  Thrust up sharp peaks to tear the tender sky.
'No more to do but hear that English chime'
  I to a kinsman wrote.   He made reply,
'As home I bring my girl and boy full soon,
I pass through Evesham, — meet me there at noon.

'The bells your father loved you needs must hear,
  Seek Oxford next with me,' and told the day.
'Upon the bridge I'll meet you.   What! how dear
  Soever was a dream, shall it bear sway
To mar the waking?'
                      I set forth, drew near,
  Beheld a goodly tower, twin churches grey,
Evesham.   The bridge, and noon.   I nothing knew
What to my heart that fateful chime would do.

For suddenly the sweet bells overcame
  A world unsouled; did all with man endow;
His yearning almost tell that passeth name
  And said they were full old, and they were now
And should be; and their sighing upon the same
  For our poor sake that pass they did avow,
While on clear Avon flowed like man's short day
The shining river of life lapsing away.

The stroke of noon. The bell-bird! yes and no.
   Winds of remembrance swept as over the foam
Of anti-natal shores. At home is it so,
   My country folk? Ay, 'neath this pale blue dome,
Many of you in the moss lie low — lie low.
   Ah! since I have not HER, give me too, home.
A footstep near! I turned; past likelihood,
Past hope, before me on the bridge — SHE STOOD.

A rosy urchin had her hand; this cried,
   'We think you are our cousin — yes, you are;
I said so to Estelle.' The violet-eyed,
   'If this be Geoffrey?' asked; and as from far
A doubt came floating up; but she denied
   Her thought, yet blushed. O beautiful! my Star!
Then, with the lifting of my hat, each wore
That look which owned to each, 'We have met before.'

Then was the strangest bliss in life made mine;
   I saw the almost worshipped — all remote;
The Star so high above that used to shine,
   Translated from the void where it did float,
And brought into relation with the fine
   Charities earth hath grown. A great joy smote
Me silent, and the child atween us tway,
We watched the lucent river stealing away.

While her deep eyes down on the ripple fell,
    Quoth the small imp, ' " How fast you go and go,
You Avon.   Does it wish to stop, Estelle,
    And hear the clock, and see the orchards blow ?
It does not care !   Not when the old big bell
    Makes a great buzzing noise ? — Who told you so ? "
And then to me, " I like to hear it hum.
Why do you think that father could not come ?

Estelle forgot her violin.   And he,
    O then he said : " How careless, child, of you ;
I must send on for it.   'T would pity be
    If that were lost."
                        I want to learn it too ;
And when I 'm nine I shall."
                        Then turning, she
    Let her sweet eyes unveil them to my view ;
Her stately grace outmatched my dream of old,
But ah ! the smile dull memory had not told.

My kinsman next, with care-worn kindly brow.
    ' Well, father,' quoth the imp, ' we 've done our part.
We found him.'
                    And she, wholly girlish now,
    Laid her young hand on his with lovely art
And sweet excuses.   O ! I made my vow
    I would all dare, such life did warm my heart ;

We journeyed, all the air with scents of price
Was laden, and the goal was Paradise.

When that the Moors betook them to their sand,
  Their domination over in fair Spain,
Each locked, men say, his door in that loved land,
  And took the key in hope to come again.
On Moorish walls yet hung, long dust each hand,
  The keys, but not the might to use, remain ;
Is there such house in some blest land for me ?
I can, I will, I do reach down the key.

A country conquered oft, and long before,
  Of generations aye ordained to win ;
If mine the power, I will unlock the door.
  Enter, O light, I bear a sunbeam in.
What, did the crescent wane ! Yet man is more,
  And love achieves because to heaven akin.
O life ! to hear again that wandering bell,
And hear it at thy feet, Estelle, Estelle.

Full oft I want the sacred throated bird,
  Over our limitless waste of light which spoke
The spirit of the call my fathers heard,
  Saying ' Let us pray,' and old world echoes woke
Ethereal minster bells that still averr'd,
  And with their phantom notes th' all silence broke.

' The fanes are far, but whom they shrined is near.
Thy God, the Island God, is here, is here.'

To serve ; to serve a thought, and serve apart
   To meet ; a few short days, a maiden won.
' Ah, sweet, sweet home, I must divide my heart,
   Betaking me to countries of the sun.'
' What straight-hung leaves, what rays that twinkle and
      dart,
   Make me to like them.'
               ' Love, it shall be done.'
' What weird dawn-fire across the wide hill flies.'
' It is the flame-tree's challenge to yon scarlet skies.'

' Hark, hark, O hark ! the spirit of a bell !
   What would it ? (' Toll.') An air-hung sacred call,
Athwart the forest shade it strangely fell ' —
   ' Toll ' — ' Toll.'
            The longed-for voice, but ah, withal
I felt, I knew, it was my father's knell
   That touched and could the over-sense enthrall.
Perfect his peace, a whispering pure and deep
As theirs who 'neath his native towers by Avon sleep.

If love and death are ever reconciled,
   'T is when the old lie down for the great rest.
We rode across the bush, a sylvan wild
   That was an almost world, whose calm oppressed

With audible silence; and great hills inisled
    Rose out as from a sea.   Consoling, blest
And blessing spoke she, and the reedflower spread,
And tall rock lilies towered above her head.

———

Sweet is the light aneath our matchless blue,
    The shade below yon passion plant that lies,
And very sweet is love, and sweet are you,
    My little children dear, with violet eyes,
And sweet about the dawn to hear anew
    The sacred monotone of peace arise.
Love, 't is thy welcome from the air-hung bell,
Congratulant and clear, Estelle, Estelle.

———

LOSS AND WASTE.

UP to far Osteroe and Suderoe
    The deep sea-floor lies strewn with Spanish wrecks,
O'er minted gold the fair-haired fishers go,
    O'er sunken bravery of high carvèd decks.

In earlier days great Carthage suffered bale
    (All her waste works choke under sandy shoals);
And reckless hands tore down the temple veil;
    And Omar burned the Alexandrian rolls.

The Old World arts men suffered not to last,
  Flung down they trampled lie and sunk from view,
He lets wild forest for these ages past
  Grow over the lost cities of the New.

O for a life that shall not be refused
To see the lost things found, and waste things used.

———◦◦◦———

ON A PICTURE.

AS a forlorn soul waiting by the Styx
  Dimly expectant of lands yet more dim,
Might peer afraid where shadows change and mix
  Till the dark ferryman shall come for him.

And past all hope a long ray in his sight,
  Fall'n trickling down the steep crag Hades-black
Reveals an upward path to life and light,
  Nor any let but he should mount that track.

As with the sudden shock of joy amazed,
  He might a motionless sweet moment stand,
So doth that mortal lover, silent, dazed, .
  For hope had died and loss was near at hand.

'Wilt thou?' his quest. Unready but for 'Nay,'
He stands at fault for joy, she whispering 'Ay.'

THE SLEEP OF SIGISMUND.

The **doom'd king pacing all night through the windy fallow.**
' Let me alone, mine enemy, let me alone,'
Never a Christian bell that dire thick gloom to hallow,
Or guide him, shelterless, succourless, thrust from his own.

Foul spirits riding the wind do flout at him friendless,
The rain and the storm on his head beat ever at will ;
His weird is on him to grope in the dark with endless
Weariful feet for a goal that shifteth still.

A sleuth-hound baying ! The sleuth-hound bayeth be-
    hind him,   .
His head, he flying and stumbling turns back to the sound,
Whom doth the sleuth-hound follow ? What if it find
    him ;
Up ! for the scent lieth thick. up from the level ground.

Up. on, he must on, to follow his weird essaying,
Lo you, a flood from the crag cometh raging past,
He falls, he fights in the water, no stop, no staying,
Soon the king's head goes under, the weird is dreed at
    last.

'Wake, O king, the best star worn
In the crown of night, forlorn
Blinks a fine white point — 't is morn.'
Soft! The queen's voice, fair is she,
'Wake!' He waketh, living, free,
In the chamber of arras lieth he.
Delicate dim shadows yield
Silken curtains over head
All abloom with work of neeld,
Martagon and milleflower spread.
On the wall his golden shield,
Dinted deep in battle field,
When the host o' the Khalif fled.
Gold to gold Long sunbeams flit
Upward, tremble and break on it.
'Ay, 't is over, all things writ
Of my sleep shall end awake,
Now is joy, and all its bane
The dark shadow of after pain.'
Then the queen saith, 'Nay, but break
Unto me for dear love's sake
This thy matter. Thou hast been
In great bitterness I ween
All the night-time.' But 'My queen,
Life, love, lady, rest content,
Ill dreams fly, the night is spent,

Good day draweth on.   Lament
'Vaileth not, — yea peace,' quoth he ;
' Sith this thing no better may be,
Best were held 'twixt thee and me.'
Then the fair queen, ' Even so
As thou wilt, O king, but know
Mickle nights have wrought thee woe,
Yet the last was troubled sore
Above all that went before.'
Quoth the king, ' No more, no more.'
Then he riseth, pale of blee,
As one spent, and utterly
Master'd of dark destiny.

II.

Comes a day for glory famed
Tidings brought the enemy shamed,
Fallen ; now is peace proclaimed.
And a swarm of bells on high
Make their sweet din scale the sky,
' Hail ! hail ! hail ! ' the people cry
To the king his queen beside,
And the knights in armour ride
After until eventide.

III.

All things great may life afford,
Praise, power, love, high pomp, fair gaud,

Till the banquet be toward
Hath this king. Then day takes flight,
Sinketh sun and fadeth light,
Late he coucheth — Night; 't is night.

The proud king heading the host on his red-roan charger.
Dust. On a thicket of spears glares the Syrian sun,
The Saracens swarm to the onset, larger aye larger
    Loom their fierce cohorts, they shout as the day were
        won.

Brown faces fronting the steel-bright armour, and ever
    The crash o' the combat runs on with a mighty cry,
Fell tumult; trampling and carnage — then fails en-
        deavour,
    O shame upon shame — the Christians falter and fly.

The foe upon them, the foe afore and behind them,
    The king borne back in the mêlée; all, all is vain:
They fly with death at their heels, fierce sun-rays blind
        them,
    Riderless steeds affrighted, tread down their ranks
        amain.

Disgrace, dishonour, no rally, ah no retrieving,
    The scorn of scorns shall his name and his nation
        brand,

'T is a sword that smites from the rear, his helmet
    cleaving,
  That hurls him to earth, to his death on the desert
    sand.

Ever they fly, the cravens, and ever reviling
  Flies after. Athirst, ashamèd, he yieldeth his breath,
While one looks down from his charger; and calm slow
    smiling,
  Curleth his lip. 'T is the Khalif. And this is death.

IV.

'Wake, yon purple peaks arise,
Jagged, bare, through saffron skies;
Now is heard a twittering sweet,
For the mother-martins meet,
Where wet ivies, dew-besprent,
Glisten on the battlement.
Now the lark at heaven's gold gate
Aiming, sweetly chides on fate
That his brown wings wearied were
When he, sure, was almost there.
Now the valley mist doth break,
Shifting sparkles edge the lake,
Love, Lord, Master, wake, O wake!'

v.

Ay, he wakes, — and dull of cheer,
Though this queen be very dear,
Though a respite come with day
From th' abhorrèd flight and fray,
E'en though life be not the cost,
Nay, nor crown nor honour lost;
For in his soul abideth fear
Worse than of the Khalif's spear,
Smiting when perforce in flight
He was borne, — for that was night,
That his weird.   But now 't is day,
'And good sooth I know not — nay,
Know not how this thing could be.
Never, more it seemeth me
Than when left the weird to dree,
I am I.   And it was I
Felt or ever they turned to fly,
How, like wind, a tremor ran,
The right hand of every man
Shaking.   Ay, all banners shook,
And the red all cheeks forsook,
Mine as theirs.   Since this was I,
Who my soul shall certify
When again I face the foe
Manful courage shall not go.

Ay, it is not thrust o' a spear,
Scorn of infidel eyes austere,
But mine own fear — is to fear.'

VI.

After sleep thus sore bestead,
Beaten about and buffeted,
Featly fares the morning spent
In high sport and tournament.

VII.

Served within his sumptuous tent,
Looks the king in quiet wise,
Till this fair queen yield the prize
To the bravest; but when day
Falleth to the west away,
Unto her i' the silent hour,
While she sits in her rose-bower.
Come, 'O love, full oft,' quoth she,
' I at dawn have prayèd thee
Thou would'st tell o' the weird to me,
Sith I might some counsel find
Of my wit or in my mind
Thee to better.'   'Ay, e'en so,
But the telling shall let thee know,'
Quoth the king, ' is neither scope

For sweet counsel nor fair hope,
Nor is found for respite room,
Till the uttermost crack of doom.

VIII.

Then the queen saith, 'Woman's wit
No man asketh aid of it,
Not wild hyssop on a wall
Is of less account; or small
Glossy gnats that flit i' the sun
Less worth weighing — light so light!
Yet when all 's said — ay, all done,
Love, I love thee! By love's might
I will counsel thee aright,
Or would share the weird to-night.'
Then he answer'd, 'Have thy way.
Know 't is two years gone and a day
Since I, walking lone and late,
Ponder'd sore mine ill estate ;
Open murmurers, foes concealed,
Famines dire i' the marches round,
Neighbour kings unfriendly found,
Ay, and treacherous plots revealed
Where I trusted. I bid stay
All my knights at the high crossway,
And did down the forest fare
To bethink me, and despair.

'Ah! thou gilded toy a throne,
If one mounts to thee alone,
Quoth I, mourning while I went,
Haply he may drop content
As a lark wing-weary down
To the level, and his crown
Leave for another man to don;
Throne, thy gold steps raised upon.
But for me — O as for me
What is named I would not dree,
Earn, or conquer, or forego
For the barring of overthrow.'

IX.

'Aloud I spake, but verily
Never an answer looked should be.
But it came to pass from shade
Pacing to an open glade,
Which the oaks a mighty wall
Fence about, methought a call
Sounded, then a pale thin mist
Rose, a pillar, and fronted me,
Rose and took a form I wist,
And it wore a hood on 'ts head,
And a long white garment spread,
And I saw the eyes thereof.

X.

Then my plumèd cap I doff,
Stooping. 'T is the white-witch. 'Hail,'
Quoth the witch, 'thou shalt prevail
An thou wilt; I swear to thee
All thy days shall glorious shine,
Great and rich, ay, fair and fine,
So what followeth rest my fee,
So thou'lt give thy sleep to me.'

XI.

While she spake my heart did leap.
Waking is man's life, and sleep —
What is sleep? — a little death
Coming after, and methought
Life is mine and death is nought
Till it come, — so day is mine
I will risk the sleep to shine
In the waking.
                     And she saith,
In a soft voice clear and low,
'Give thy plumèd cap also
For a token.'
                     'Didst thou give?'
Quoth the queen; and 'As I live
He makes answer 'none can tell.
I did will my sleep to sell,

And in token held to her
That she askèd.   And it fell
To the grass.   I saw no stir
In her hand or in her face,
And no going ; but the place
Only for an evening mist
Was made empty.   There it lay,
That same plumèd cap, alway
On the grasses — but I wist
Well, it must be let to lie,
And I left it.   Now the tale
Ends, th' events do testify
Of her truth.   The days go by
Better and better ; nought doth ail
In the land, right happy and hale
Dwell the seely folk ; but sleep
Brings a reckoning ; then forth creep
Dreaded creatures, worms of might.
Crested with my plumèd cap
Loll about my neck all night,
Bite me in the side, and lap
My heart's blood.   Then oft the weird
Drives me, where amazed, afeard,
I do safe on a river strand
Mark one sinking hard at hand
While fierce sleuth-hounds that me track
Fly upon me, bear me back,
Fling me away, and he for lack

Of man's aid in piteous wise
Goeth under, drowns and dies

XII.

' O sweet wife, I suffer sore —
O methinks aye more and more
Dull my day, my courage numb,
Shadows from the night to come.
But no counsel, hope, nor aid
Is to give ; a crown being made
Power and rule, yea all good things
Yet to hang on this same weird
I must dree it, ever that brings
Chastening from the white-witch feared.
O that dreams mote me forsake,
Would that man could alway wake.'

XIII.

Now good sooth doth counsel fail,
Ah this queen is pale, so pale.
' Love,' she sigheth, ' thou didst not well
Listening to the white-witch fell,
Leaving her doth thee advance
Thy plumèd cap of maintenance.'

XIV.

' She is white, as white snow flake,'
Quoth the king ; ' a man shall make

Bargains with her and not sin.'
'Ay,' she saith, ' but an he win,
Let him look the right be done
Else the rue shall be his own.

XV.

No more words. The stars are bright,
For the feast high halls be dight
Late he coucheth.   Night — 't is night.

The dead king lying in state in the Minster holy.
Fifty candles burn at his head and burn at his feet,
A crown and royal apparel upon him lorn and lowly,
  And the cold hands stiff as horn by their cold palms
    meet.

Two days dead. Is he dead?   Nay, nay — but is he
    living?
The weary monks have ended their chantings manifold,
The great door swings behind them, night winds entrance
    giving,
  The candles flare and drip on him, warm and he so cold.

Neither to move nor to moan, though sunk and though
    swallow'd
  In earth he shall soon be trodden hard and no more
    seen.

Soft you the door again !   Was it a footstep followed,
  Falter'd, and yet drew near him ? — Malva, Malva the
    queen !

One hand o' the dead king liveth (e'en so him seemeth)
  On the purple robe, on the ermine that folds his breast
Cold, very cold.   Yet e'en at that pass esteemeth
  The king, it were sweet if she kissed the place of its rest.

Laid her warm face on his bosom, a fair wife grievèd
  For the lord and love of her youth, and bewailed him
    sore ;
Laid her warm face on the bosom of her bereavèd
  Soon to go under, never to look on her more.

His candles guide her with pomp funereal flaring,
  Out of the gulfy dark to the bier whereon he lies.
Cometh this queen i' the night for grief or for daring,
  Out o' the dark to the light with large affrighted eyes ?

The pale queen speaks in the Presence with fear upon
    her,
  'Where is the ring I gave to thee, where is my ring ?
I vowed — 't was an evil vow — by love, and by honour,
  Come life or come death to be thine, thou poor dead
    king.'

The pale queen's honour! A low laugh scathing and
    sereing —
  A mumbling as made by the dead in the tombs ye
    wot.
Braveth the dead this queen? 'Hear it, whoso hath
    hearing,
  I vowed by my love, cold king, but I loved thee not.'

Honour!   An echo in aisles and the solemn portals,
  Low sinketh this queen by the bier with its freight for-
    lorn ;
Yet kneeling, 'Hear me!' she crieth, 'you just immor-
    tals,
  You saints bear witness I vowed and am not forsworn.

I vowed in my youth, fool-king, when the golden fetter
  Thy love that bound me and bann'd me full weary I
    wore,
But all poor men of thy menai I held them better,
  All stalwart knights of thy train unto me were more.

Twenty years I have lived on earth and two beside thee,
  Thirty years thou didst live on earth, and two on the
    throne :
Let it suffice there be none of thy rights denied thee,
  Though I dare thy presence — I — come for my ring
    alone.'

She risen shuddereth, peering, afraid to linger
    Behold her ring, it shineth! 'Now yield to me, thou
      dead,
For this do I dare the touch of thy stark stiff finger.'
    The queen hath drawn her ring from his hand, the
      queen hath fled.

'O woman fearing sore, to whom my man's heart cleavèd,
    The faith enwrought with love and life hath mocks for
      its meed ' —
The dead king lying in state, of his past bereavèd,
    Twice dead. Ay, this is death. Now dieth the king
      indeed.

XVI.

    ' Wake, the seely gnomes do fly,
    Drenched across yon rainy sky,
    With the vex'd moon-mother'd elves,
    And the clouds do weep themselves
    Into morning.
             All night long
    Hath thy weird thee sore opprest;
    Wake, I have found within my breast
    Counsel.' Ah, the weird was strong,
    But the time is told. Release
    Openeth on him when his eyes
    Lift them in dull desolate wise,
    And behold he is at peace.

10

Ay, but silent.   Of all done
And all suffer'd in the night,
Of all ills that do him spite
She shall never know that one.
Then he heareth accents bland,
Seeth the queen's ring on his hand,
And he riseth calmed withal.

XVII.

Rain and wind on the palace wall
Beat and bluster, sob and moan,
When at noon he musing lone,
Comes the queen anigh his seat,
And she kneeleth at his feet.

XVIII.

Quoth the queen, 'My love, my lord,
Take thy wife and take thy sword,
We must forth in the stormy weather,
Thou and I to the witch together.
Thus I rede thee counsel deep,
Thou didst ill to sell thy sleep,
Turning so man's wholesome life
From its meaning.   Thine intent
None shall hold for innocent.
Thou dost take thy good things first,
Then thou art cast into the worst;

First the glory, then the strife.
Nay, but first thy trouble dree,
So thy peace shall sweeter be.
First to work and then to rest,
Is the way for our humanity,
Ay, she sayeth that loves thee best,
We must forth and from this strife
Buy the best part of man's life ;
Best and worst thou holdest still
Subject to a witch's will.
Thus I rede thee counsel deep,
Thou didst ill to sell thy sleep ;
Take the crown from off thy head,
Give it the white-witch instead,
If in that she say thee nay,
Get the night, — and give the day.'

XIX.

Then the king (amazèd, mild,
As one reasoning with a child
All his speech) : 'My wife ! my fair !
And his hand on her brown hair
Trembles ; 'Lady, dost indeed
Weigh the meaning of thy rede ?
Would'st thou dare the dropping away
Of allegiance, should our sway
And sweet splendour and renown
All be risked ? (methinks a crown

Doth become thee marvellous well).
We ourself are, truth to tell,
Kingly both of wont and kind,
Suits not such the craven mind.'
' Yet this weird thou can'st not dree.'
Quoth the queen, ' And live ; ' then he,
' I must die and leave the fair
Unborn, long-desired heir
To his rightful heritage.'

XX.

But this queen arisen doth high
Her two hands uplifting, sigh
' God forbid.'   And he to assuage
Her keen sorrow, for his part
Searcheth, nor can find in his heart
Words.   And weeping she will rest
Her sweet cheek upon his breast,
Whispering, ' Dost thou verily
Know thou art to blame ?   Ah me,
Come,' and yet beseecheth she,
' Ah me, come.'
                        For good for ill,
Whom man loveth hath her will.
Court and castle left behind,
Stolen forth in the rain and wind,
Soon they are deep in the forest, fain
The white-witch to raise again ;

Down and deep where flat o'erhead
Layer on layer do cedars spread,
Down where lordly maples strain,
Wrestling with the storm amain.

XXI.

Wide-wing'd eagles struck on high
Headlong fall'n break through, and lie
With their prey in piteous wise,
And no film on their dead eyes.
Matted branches grind and crash,
Into darkness dives the flash,
Stabs, a dread gold dirk of fire,
Loads the lift with splinters dire.
Then a pause i' the deadly feud —
And a sick cowed quietude.

XXII.

Soh! A pillar misty and grey,
'T is the white-witch in the way.
Shall man deal with her and gain?
I trow not. Albeit the twain
Costly gear and gems and gold
Freely offer, she will hold
Sleep and token for the pay
She did get for greatening day.

XXIII.

'Or the night shall rest my fee
Or the day shall nought of me,'
Quoth the witch.   'An't thee beseem,
Sell thy kingdom for a dream.'

XXIV.

'Now what will be let it be!'
Quoth the queen; 'but choose the right.'
And the white-witch scorns at her,
Stately standing in their sight.
Then without or sound or stir
She is not.   For offering meet
Lieth the token at their feet,
Which they, weary and sore bestead
In the storm, lift up, full fain
Ere the waning light hath fled
Those high towers they left to gain.

XXV.

Deep among tree roots astray
Here a torrent tears its way,
There a cedar split aloft
Lies head downward.   Now the oft
Muttering thunder, now the wind
Wakens.   How the path to find?

How the turning? Deep ay deep,
Far ay far. She needs must weep,
This fair woman, lost, astray
In the forest; nought to say.
Yet the sick thoughts come and go,
' I, 't was I would have it so.'

XXVI.

Shelter at the last, a roof
Wrought of ling (in their behoof,
Foresters, that drive the deer).
What, and must they couch them here?
Ay, and ere the twilight fall
Gather forest berries small
And nuts down beaten for a meal.

XXVII.

Now the shy wood-wonners steal
Nearer, bright-eyed furry things,
Winking owls on silent wings
Glance, and float away. The light
In the wake o' the storm takes flight,
Day departeth: night — 't is night

The crown'd king musing at morn by a clear sweet river.
Palms on the slope o' the valley, and no winds blow;
Birds blameless, dove-eyed, mystical talk deliver,
Oracles haply. The language he doth not know.

Bare, blue, are yon peakèd hills for a rampart lying,
  As dusty gold is the light in the palms o'erhead,
'What is the name o' the land? and this calm sweet
    sighing,
  If it be echo, where first was it caught and spread?

I might — I might be at rest in some field Elysian,
  If this be asphodel set in the herbage fair,
I know not how I should wonder, so sweet the vision,
  So clear and silent the water, the field, the air.

Love, are you by me! Malva, what think you this
    meaneth?
  Love, do you see the fine folk as they move over there?
Are they immortals? Look you a wingèd one leaneth
  Down from yon pine to the river of us unaware.

All unaware; and the country is full of voices,
  Mild strangers passing: they reck not of me nor of thee.
List! about and around us wondrous sweet noises,
  Laughter of little children and maids that dreaming be.

Love, I can see their dreams.' A dim smile flitteth
  Over her lips, and they move as in peace supreme,
And a small thing, silky haired, beside her sitteth,
  'O this is thy dream atween us — this is thy dream.'

Was it then truly his dream with her dream that blended?
'Speak, dear child dear,' quoth the queen, 'and mine
  own little son.'
' Father,' the small thing murmurs; then all is ended,
  He starts from that passion of peace — ay, the dream is
  done.

XXVIII.

' I have been in a good land,'
Quoth the king: ' O sweet sleep bland,
Blessed! I am grown to more,
Now the doing of right hath moved
Me to love of right, and proved
If one doth it, he shall be
Twice the man he was before.
Verily and verily,
Thou fair woman, thou didst well;
I look back and scarce may tell
Those false days of tinsel sheen,
Flattery, feasting, that have been.
Shows of life that were but shows,
How they held me; being I ween
Like sand-pictures thin, that rose
Quivering, when our thirsty bands
Marched i' the hot Egyptian lands;
Shade of palms on a thick green plot,
Pools of water that was not,
Mocking us and melting away.

XXIX.

I have been a witch's prey,
Art mine enemy now by day,
Thou fell Fear? There comes an end
To the day ; thou canst not wend
After me where I shall fare,
My foredoomèd peace to share.
And awake with a better heart,
I shall meet thee and take my part
O' the dull world's dull spite ; with thine
Hard will I strive for me and mine.'

XXX.

A page and a palfrey pacing nigh,
Malva the queen awakes.   A sigh —
One amazèd moment — 'Ay,
We remember yesterday,
Let us to the palace straight :
What! do all my ladies wait —
Is no zeal to find me?   What!
No knights forth to meet the king ;
Due observance, is it forgot?'

XXXI.

'Lady,' quoth the page, 'I bring
Evil news.   Sir king, I say,

My good lord of yesterday,
Evil news.' This king saith low,
'Yesterday, and yesterday, ⋆
The queen's yesterday we know,
Tell us thine.' 'Sir king,' saith he,
Hear. Thy castle in the night
Was surprised, and men thy flight
Learned but then; thine enemy
Of old days, our new king, reigns;
And sith thou wert not at pains
To forbid it, hear alsò,
Marvelling whereto this should grow
How thy knights at break of morn
Have a new allegiance sworn,
And the men-at-arms rejoice,
And the people give their voice
For the conqueror. I, Sir king,
Rest thine only friend. I bring
Means of flight; now therefore fly,
A great price is on thy head.
Cast her jewel'd mantle by,
Mount thy queen i' the selle and hie
(Sith disguise ye need, and bread)
Down yon pleachèd track, down, down,
Till a tower shall on thee frown;
Him that holds it show this ring:
So farewell, my lord the king.'

XXXII.

Had one marked that palfrey led
To the tower, he sooth had said,
These are royal folk and rare —
Jewels in her plaited hair
Shine not clearer than her eyes,
And her lord in goodly wise
With his plumèd cap in 's hand
Moves in the measure of command.

XXXIII.

Had one marked where stole forth two
From the friendly tower anew,
'Common folk ' he sooth had said,
Making for the mountain track.
Common, common, man and maid,
Clad in russet, and of kind
Meet for russet.   On his back
A wallet bears the stalwart hind;
She, all shy, in rustic grace
Steps beside her man apace,
And wild roses match her face.

XXXIV.

Whither speed they ?   Where are toss'd
Like sea foam the dwarfèd pines
At the jagged sharp inclines ;

To the country of the frost
Up the mountains to be lost,
Lost.   No better now may be,
Lost where mighty hollows thrust
'Twixt the fierce teeth of the world,
Fill themselves with crimson dust
When the tumbling sun down hurl'd
Stares among them drearily,
As a' wondering at the lone
Gulfs that weird gaunt company
Fenceth in   Lost there unknown,
Lineage, nation, name, and throne.

XXXV.

Lo, in a crevice choked with ling
And fir, this man, not now the king,
This Sigismund, hath made a fire,
And by his wife in the dark night
He leans at watch, her guard and squire.
His wide eyes stare out for the light
Weary.   He needs must chide on fate,
And she is asleep.   'Poor brooding mate,
What! wilt thou on the mountain crest
Slippery and cold scoop thy first nest?
Or must I clear some uncouth cave
That lair'd the mother wolf, and save —
Spearing her cubs — the grey pelt fine
To be a bed for thee and thine?

It is my doing.   Ay,' quoth he,
' Mine ; but who dares to pity thee
Shall pity, not for loss of all,
But that thou wert my wife perdie,
E'en wife unto a witch's thrall, —
A man beholden to the cold
Cloud for a covering, he being sold
And hunted for reward of gold.

XXXVI.

But who shall chronicle the ways
Of common folk — the nights and days
Spent with rough goatherds on their snows,
Of travellers come whence no man knows,
Then gone aloft on some sharp height
In the dumb peace and the great light
Amid brown eagles and wild roes ?

XXXVII.

'T is the whole world whereon they lie,
The rocky pastures hung on high
Shelve off upon an empty sky.
But they creep near the edge, look down —
Great heaven ! another world afloat,
Moored as in seas of air ; remote
As their own childhood ; swooning away
Into a tenderer sweeter day,

Innocent, sunny. 'O for wings!
There lie the lands of other kings —
I, Sigismund, my sometime crown
Forfeit; forgotten of renown
My wars, my rule; I fain would go
Down to yon peace obscure.'

      Even so;
Down to the country of the thyme,
Where young kids dance, and a soft chime
Of sheepbells tinkles; then at last
Down to a country of hollows, cast
Up at the mountains full of trees,
Down to fruit orchards and wide leas,

XXXVIII.

With name unsaid and fame unsunned
He walks that was King Sigismund.
With palmers holy and pilgrims brown,
New from the East, with friar and clown,
He mingles in a wallèd town,
And in the mart where men him scan
He passes for a merchant man.
For from his vest, where by good hap
He thrust it, he his plumèd cap
Hath drawn and plucked the gems away,
And up and down he makes essay
To sell them; they are all his wares
And wealth. He is a man of cares,

A man of toil; no roof hath he
To shelter her full soon to be
The mother of his dispossessed
Desirèd heir.

XXXIX.

Few words are best.
He, once King Sigismund, saith few,
But makes good diligence and true.
Soon with the gold he gather'd so,
A little homestead lone and low
He buyeth : a field, a copse, with these
A melon patch and mulberry trees.
And is the man content?   Nay, morn
Is toilsome, oft is noon forlorn,
Though right be done and life be won,
Yet hot is weeding in the sun,
Yea scythe to wield and axe to swing,
Are hard on sinews of a king.

XL.

And Malva, must she toil?   E'en so.
Full patiently she takes her part,
All, all so new.   But her deep heart
Forebodes more change than shall be shown
Betwixt a settle and a throne.
And lost in musing she will go

About the winding of her silk,
About the skimming her goat's milk,
About the kneading of her bread,
And water drawn from her well-head.

XLI.

Then come the long nights dark and still,
Then come the leaves and cover the sill,
Then come the swift flocks of the stare,
Then comes the snow — then comes the heir.

XLII.

If he be glad, if he be sad,
How should one question when the hand
Is full, the heart. That life he had,
While leisure was aside may stand,
Till he shall overtake the task
Of every day, then let him ask
(If he remember — if he will),
' When I could sit me down and muse,
And match my good against mine ill,
And weigh advantage dulled by use
At nothing, was it better with me ? '
But Sigismund ! It cannot be
But that he toil, nor pause, nor sigh,
A dreamer on a day gone by
The king is come.

11

XLIII.

His vassals two
Serve with all homage deep and due.
He is contented, he doth find
Belike the kingdom much to his mind.
And when the long months of his long
Reign are two years, and like a song
From some far sweeter world, a call
From the king's mouth for fealty,
Buds soon to blossom in language fall,
They listen and find not any plea
Left, for fine chiding at destiny.

XLIV.

Sigismund hath ricked the hay,
He sitteth at close o' a sultry day
Under his mulberry boughs at ease.
' Hey for the world, and the world is wide,
The world is mine, and the world is — these
Beautiful Malva leans at his side,
And the small babbler talks at his knees.

XLV.

Riseth a waft as of summer air,
Floating upon it what moveth there?
Faint as the light of stars and wan
As snow at night when the moon is gone,
It is the white-witch risen once more.

XLVI.

The white witch that tempted of yore
So utterly doth substance lack,
You may breathe her nearer and breathe her back.
Soft her eyes, her speech full clear:
' Hail, thou Sigismund my fere,
Bargain with me yea or nay.
NAY, I go to my true place,
And no more thou seest my face.
YEA, the good be all thine own,
For now will I advance thy day,
And yet will leave the night alone.

XLVII.

Sigismund makes answer ' NAY.
Though the Highest heaped on me
Trouble, yet the same should be
Welcomer than weal from thee.
Nay ; — for ever and ever Nay.'
O, the white-witch floats away.
Look you, look ! A still pure smile
Blossoms on her mouth the while,
White wings peakèd high behind,
Bear her ; — no, the wafting wind,
For they move not, — floats her back,
Floats her up. They scarce may track

Her swift rising, shot on high
Like a ray from the western sky,
Or a lark from some grey wold
Utterly whelm'd in sunset gold,

XLVIII.

Then these two long silence hold,
And the lisping babe doth say
'White white bird, it flew away.'
And they marvel at these things,
For her ghostly visitings
Turn to them another face.
Haply she was sent, a friend
Trying them, and to good end
For their better weal and grace;
One more wonder let to be
In the might and mystery
Of the world, where verily
And good sooth a man may wend
All his life, and no more view
Than the one right next to do.

XLIX.

So, the welcome dusk is here,
Sweet is even, rest is dear;
Mountain heads have lost the light,
Soon they couch them. Night — 't is night.

Sigismund dreaming delightsomely after his haying.
    ('Sleep of the labouring man,' quoth King David, 'is
      sweet.')
'Sigismund, Sigismund'—'Who is this calling and saying
    "Sigismund, Sigismund," O blessed night do not fleet.

Is it not dark—ay, methinks it is dark, I would slumber,
    O I would rest till the swallow shall chirp 'neath mine
      eaves.'
'Sigismund, Sigismund,' multitudes now without number
    Calling, the noise is as dropping of rain upon leaves.

'Ay,' quoth he dreaming, 'say on, for I, Sigismund,
    hear ye.'
'Sigismund, Sigismund, all the knights weary full sore.
Come back, King Sigismund, come, they shall love thee
    and fear thee,
    The people cry out O come back to us, reign ever-
      more.

The new king is dead, and we will not his son, no nor
    brother,
    Come with thy queen, is she busy yet, kneading of
      cakes?
Sigismund, show us the boy, is he safe, and his mother,
    Sigismund?'—dreaming he falls into laughter and
      wakes.

L.

And men say this dream came true,
For he walking in the dew
Turned aside while yet was red
On the highest mountain head,
Looking how the wheat he set
Flourished.　And the knights him met
And him prayèd 'Come again,
Sigismund our king, and reign.'
But at first — at first they tell
How it liked not Malva well;
She must leave her belted bees
And the kids that she did rear.
When she thought on it full dear
Seemed her home.　It did not please
Sigismund that he must go
From the wheat that he did sow;
When he thought on it his mind
Was not that should any bind
Into sheaves that wheat but he,
Only he; and yet they went,
And it may be were content.
And they won a nation's heart;
Very well they played their part.
They ruled with sceptre and diadem,
And their children after them.

THE MAID-MARTYR.

ONLY you 'd have me speak.
      Whether to speak
Or whether to be silent is all one ;
Whether to sleep and in my dreaming front
Her small scared face forlorn ; whether to wake
And muse upon her small soft feet that paced
The hated, hard, inhospitable stone —
I say all 's one. But you would have me speak,
And change one sorrow for the other. Ay,
Right reverend father, comfortable father,
Old, long in thrall, and wearied of the cell,
So will I here — here staring through the grate,
Whence, sheer beneath us lying the little town,
Her street appears a riband up the rise ;
Where 't is right steep for carts, behold two ruts
Worn in the flat, smooth, stone.
      That side I stood ;
My head was down. At first I did but see
Her coming feet ; they gleamed through my hot tears
As she walked barefoot up yon short steep hill.
Then I dared all, gazed on her face, the maid
Martyr and utterly, utterly broke my heart.

Her face, O! it was wonderful to me,
There was not in it what I look'd for — no,
I never saw a maid go to her death,
How should I dream that face and the dumb soul?

Her arms and head were bare, seemly she walked
All in her smock so modest as she might;
Upon her shoulders hung a painted cape
For horrible adornment, flames of fire
Portrayed upon it, and mocking demon heads.

Her eyes — she did not see me — opened wide,
Blue-black, gazed right before her, yet they marked
Nothing; and her two hands uplift as praying.
She yet prayed not, wept not, sighed not.   O father,
She was past that, soft, tender, hunted thing;
But, as it seemed, confused from time to time,
She would half-turn her or to left or right
To follow other streets, doubting her way.

Then their base pikes they basely thrust at her,
And, like one dazed, obedient to her guides
She came; I knew not if 't was present to her
That death was her near goal; she was so lost,
And set apart from any power to think.
But her mouth pouted as one brooding, father,
Over a lifetime of forlorn fear.   No,

Scarce was it fear; so looks a timid child
(Not more affrighted; ah! but not so pale)
That has been scolded or has lost its way.

Mother and father — father and mother kind,
She was alone, where were you hidden?   Alone,
And I that loved her more, or feared death less,
Rushed to her side, but quickly was flung back,
And cast behind o' the pikemen following her
Into a yelling and a cursing crowd,
That bristled thick with monks and hooded friars;
Moreover, women with their cheeks ablaze,
Who swarmèd after up the narrowing street.

Pitiful heaven!   I knew she did not hear
In that last hour the cursing, nor the foul
Words; she had never heard like words. sweet soul,
In her life blameless; even at that pass.
That dreadful pass, I felt it had been worse,
Though nought I longed for as for death. to know
She did.   She saw not 'neath their hoods those eyes
Soft, glittering. with a lust for cruelty;
Secret delight, that so great cruelty,
All in the sacred name of Holy Church,
Their meed to look on it should be anon.
Speak! O, I tell you this thing passeth word!

From roofs and oriels high, women looked down ;
Men, maidens, children, and a fierce white sun
Smote blinding splinters from all spears aslant.

Lo ! next a stand, so please you, certain priests
(May God forgive men sinning at their ease),
Whose duty 't was to look upon this thing,
Being mindful of thick pungent smoke to come,
Had caused a stand to rise hard by the stake,
Upon its windward side.
                                    My life ! my love !
She utter'd one sharp cry of mortal dread
While they did chain her. This thing passeth words,
Albeit told out for ever in my soul.
As the torch touched, thick volumes of black reek
Rolled out and raised the wind, and instantly
Long films of flaxen hair floated aloft,
Settled alow, in drifts upon the crowd.
The vile were merciful ; heaped high, my dear,
Thou didst not suffer long.   O ! it was soon,
Soon over, and I knew not any more,
Till grovelling on the ground, beating my head,
I heard myself, and scarcely knew 't was I,
At Holy Church railing with fierce mad words,
Crying and craving for a stake, for me.
While fast the folk, as ever, such a work
Being over, fled, and shrieked ' A heretic !
More heretics ; yon ashes smoking still.'

And up and almost over me came on
A robed — ecclesiastic — with his train
(I choose the words lest that they do some wrong)
Call him a robed ecclesiastic proud.
And I lying helpless, with my bruisèd face
Beat on his garnished shoon. But he stepped back,
Spurned me full roughly with them, called the pikes,
Delivering orders, 'Take the bruisèd wretch.
He raves. Fool! thou 'lt hear more of this anon.
Bestow him there.' He pointed to a door.
With that some threw a cloth upon my face
Because it bled. I knew they carried me
Within his home, and I was satisfied ;
Willing my death. Was it an abbey door ?
Was 't entrance to a palace ? or a house
Of priests ? I say not, nor if abbot he,
Bishop or other dignity ; enough
That he so spake. 'Take in the bruisèd wretch.'
And I was borne far up a turret stair
Into a peakèd chamber taking form
O' the roof, and on a pallet bed they left
Me miserable. Yet I knew forsooth,
Left in my pain, that evil things were said
Of that same tower ; men thence had disappeared,
Suspect of heresy had disappeared,
Deliver'd up, 't was whisper'd, tried and burned.
So be it methought, I would not live, not I.
But none did question me. A beldame old,

Kind, heedless of my sayings, tended me.
I raved at Holy Church and she was deaf,
And at whose tower detained me, she was dumb.
So had I food and water, rest and calm.
Then on the third day I rose up and sat
On the side of my low bed right melancholy,
All that high force of passion overpast,
I sick with dolourous thought and weak through tears
Spite of myself came to myself again
(For I had slept), and since I could not die
Looked through the window three parts overgrown
With leafage on the loftiest ivy ropes,
And saw at foot o' the rise another tower
In roof whereof a grating, dreary bare.
Lifetimes gone by, long, slow, dim, desolate,
I knew even there had been my lost love's cell.

So musing on the man that with his foot
Spurned me, the robed ecclesiastic stern,
' Would he had haled me straight to prison ' methought,
' So made an end at once.'
                 My sufferings rose
Like billows closing over, beating down ;
Made heavier far because of a stray, strange,
Sweet hope that mocked me at the last.
                       'T was thus,
I came from Oxford secretly, the news
Terrible of her danger smiting me, —

She was so young, and ever had been bred
With whom 't was made a peril now to name.
There had been worship in the night ; some stole
To a mean chapel deep in woods, and heard
Preaching, and prayed. She, my betrothed, was there.
Father and mother, mother and father kind,
So young, so innocent, had ye no ruth,
No fear, that ye did bring her to her doom?
I know the chiefest Evil One himself
Sanded that floor. Their footsteps marking it
Betrayed them. How all came to pass let be.
Parted, in hiding some, other in thrall,
Father and mother, mother and father kind,
It may be yet ye know not this — not all.

I in the daytime lying perdue looked up
At the castle keep impregnable, — no foot
How rash so e'er might hope to scale it. Night
Descending, come I near, perplexedness,
Contempt of danger, to the door o' the keep
Drawing me. There a short stone bench I found,
And bitterly weeping sat and leaned my head
Against the hopeless hated massiveness
Of that detested hold. A lifting moon
Had made encroachment on the dark, but deep
Was shadow where I leaned. Within a while
I was aware, but saw no shape, of one
Who stood beside me, a dark shadow tall.

I cared not, disavowal mattered nought
Of grief to one so out of love with life.
But after pause I felt a hand let down
That rested kindly, firmly, a man's hand,
Upon my shoulder; there was cheer in it.
And presently a voice clear, whispering, low,
With pitifulness that faltered, spoke to me.
Was I, it asked, true son of Mother Church?
Coldly I answer'd 'Ay;' then blessed words
That danced into mine ears more excellent
Music than wedding bells had been were said,
With certitude that I might see my maid,
My dear one. He would give a paper, he
The man beside me. 'Do thy best endeavour,
Dear youth. Thy maiden being a right sweet child
Surely will hearken to thee; an she do,
And will recant, fair faultless heretic,
Whose knowledge is but scant of matters high
Which hard men spake on with her, hard men forced
From her mouth innocent, then shall she come
Before me; have good cheer, all may be well.
But an she will not she must burn, no power —
Not Solomon the Great on 's ivory throne
With all his wisdom could find out a way,
Nor I nor any to save her, she must burn.
Now hast thou till day dawn. The Mother of God
Speed thee.' A twisted scroll he gave; himself
Knocked at the door behind, and he was gone,

A darker pillar of darkness in the dark.
Straightway one opened and I gave the scroll.
He read, then thrust it in his lanthorn flame
Till it was ashes; ' Follow' and no more
Whisper'd, went up the giddy spiring way,
I after, till we reached the topmost door.
Then took a key, opened, and crying ' Delia,
Delia my sweetheart, I am come, I am come,'
I darted forward and he locked us in.
Two figures; one rose up and ran to me
Along the ladder of moonlight on the floor,
Fell on my neck.   Long time we kissed and wept.

But for that other, while she stood appeased
For cruel parting past, locked in mine arms,
I had been glad, expecting a good end.
The cramped pale fellow prisoner ' Courage' cried.
Then Delia lifting her fair face, the moon
Did show me its incomparable calms.
Her effluent thought needed no word of mine,
It whelmed my soul as in a sea of tears.
The warm enchantment leaning on my breast
Breathed as in air remote, and I was left
To infinite detachment, even with hers
To take cold kisses from the lips of doom.
Look in those eyes and disinherit hope
From that high place late won.
                          Then murmuring low

That other spake of Him on the cross, and soft
As broken-hearted mourning of the dove,
She 'One deep calleth to another' sighed.
'The heart of Christ mourns to my heart, " Endure.
There was a day when to the wilderness
My great forerunner from his thrall sent forth
Sad messengers, demanding *Art thou He?*
Think'st thou I knew no pang in that strange hour?
How could I hold the power, and want the will
Or want the love? That pang was his — and mine.
He said not, Save me an thou be the Son,
But only *Art thou He?* In my great way
It was not writ, — legions of Angels mine,
There was one Angel, one ordain'd to unlock
At my behest the doomèd deadly door.
I could not tell him, tell not thee, why." Lord,
We know not why, but would not have Thee grieve,
Think not so deeply on 't; make us endure
For thy blest sake, hearing thy sweet voice mourn
" I will go forth, thy desolations meet,
And with my desolations solace them.
I will not break thy bonds but I am bound,
With thee." '
　　　　　　　I feared. That speech deep furrows cut
In my afflicted soul. I whisper'd low.
' Thou wilt not heed her words, my golden girl.'
But Delia said not ought; only her hand
Laid on my cheek and on the other leaned

Her own.   O there was comfort, father,
In love and nearness, e'en at the crack of doom.

Then spake I, and that other said no more,
For I appealed to God and to his Christ.
Unto the strait-barred window led my dear;
No table, bed, nor plenishing; no place
They had for rest: mangre two narrow chairs
By day, by night they sat thereon upright.
One drew I to the opening; on it set
My Delia, kneeled; upon its arm laid mine,
And prayed to God and prayed of her.

              . Father,
If you should ask e'en now, 'And art thou glad
Of what befell?' I could not say it, father,
I should be glad; therefore God make me glad,
Since we shall die to-morrow!

                Think not sin,
O holy, harmless reverend man, to fear.
'T will be soon over.   Now I know thou fear'st
Also for me, lest I be lost; but aye
Strong comfortable hope doth wrap me round,
A token of acceptance.   I am cast
From Holy Church, and not received of thine;
But the great Advocate who knoweth all,
He whispers with me.

           O my Delia wept
When I did plead; 'I have much feared to die,'

Answering. (The moonlight on her blue-black eyes
Fell; shining tears upon their lashes hung;
Fair showed the dimple that I loved; so young,
So very young.) 'But they did question me
Straitly, and make me many times to swear,
To swear of all alas, that I believed.
Truly, unless my soul I would have bound
With false oaths — difficult, innumerous, strong,
Way was not left me to get free.

       But now,'
Said she, 'I am happy; I have seen the place
Where I am going.

      I will tell it you,
Love. Hubert. Do not weep; they said to me
That you would come, and it would not be long.
Thus was it, being sad and full of fear,
I was crying in the night; and prayed to God
And said, "I have not learned high things;" and said
To the Saviour, "Do not be displeased with me,
I am not crying to get back and dwell
With my good mother and my father fond,
Nor even with my love, Hubert — my love,
Hubert; but I am crying because I fear
Mine answers were not rightly given — so hard
Those questions. If I did not understand,
Wilt thou forgive me?" And the moon went down
While I did pray, and looking on the floor,
Behold a little diamond lying there,

So small it might have dropped from out a ring.
I could but look! The diamond waxed — it grew —
It was a diamond yet. and shot out rays,
And in the midst of it a rose-red point;
It waxed till I might see the rose-red point
Was a little Angel 'mid those oval rays,
With a face sweet as the first kiss. O love,
You gave me, and it meant that self-same thing.

Now was it tall as I, among the rays
Standing; I touched not. Through the window drawn.
This barred and narrow window, — but I know
Nothing of how, we passed, and seemed to walk
Upon the air, till on the roof we sat.

It spoke. The sweet mouth did not move. but all
The Angel spoke in strange words full and old,
It was my Angel sent to comfort me
With a message, and the message, " I might come,
And myself see if He forgave me." Then
Deliver'd he admonition, " Afterwards
I must return and die." But I being dazed,
Confused with love and joy that He so far
Did condescend, " Ay, Eminence," replied,
" Is the way great ? " I knew not what I said.
The Angel then, " I know not far nor near,
But all the stars of God this side it shine."
And I forgetful wholly for this thing

My soul did pant in — a rapture and a pain,
So great as they would melt it quite away
To a vanishing like mist when sultry rays
Shot from the daystar reckon with it — I
Said in my simpleness, " But is there time?
For in three days I am to burn, and O
I would fain see that he forgiveth first.
Pray you make haste." " I know not haste," he said ;
" I was not fashioned to be thrall of time.
What is it?" And I marvelled, saw outlying,
Shaped like a shield and of dimensions like
An oval in the sky beyond all stars,
And trembled with foreknowledge. We were bound
To that same golden holy hollow. I
Misdoubted how to go, but we were gone.
I set off wingless, walking empty air
Beside him. In a moment we were caught
Among thick swarms of lost ones, evil, fell
Of might, only a little less than gods,
And strong enough to tear the earth to shreds,
Set shoulders to the sun and rend it out
O' its place. Their wings did brush across my face,
Yet felt I nought ; the place was vaster far
Than all this wholesome pastoral windy world.
Through it we spinning, pierced to its far brink,
Saw menacing frowns and we were forth again.
Time has no instant for the reckoning ought
So sudden ; 't was as if a lightning flash

Threw us within it, and a swifter flash,
We riding harmless down its swordlike edge,
Shot us fast forth to empty nothingness.

All my soul trembled, and my body it seemed
Pleaded than such a sight rather to faint
To the last silence, and the eery grave
Inhabit, and the slow solemnities
Of dying faced, content me with my shroud.

And yet was lying athwart the morning star
That shone in front, that holy hollow; yet
It loomed, as hung atilt towards the world,
That in her time of sleep appeared to look
Up to it, into it.
　　　　　　　We, though I wept,
Fearing and longing, knowing not how to go,
My heart gone first, both mine eyes dedicate
To its all-hallowed sweet desirèd gold,
We on the empty limitless abyss
Walked slowly.　It was far;
　　　　　　　　　　And I feared much,
For lo! when I looked down deep under me
The little earth was such a little thing,
How in the vasty dark find her again?
The crescent moon a moorèd boat hard by,
Did wait on her and touch her ragged rims

With a small gift of silver.

       Love! my life!
Hubert, while I yet wept, O we were there.
A menai of Angels first, a swarm of stars
Took us among them (all alive with stars
Shining and shouting each to each that place),
The feathered multitude did lie so thick
We walked upon them, walked on outspread wings,
And the great gates were standing open.

          Love!
The country is not what you think; but oh!
When you have seen it nothing else contents.
The voice, the vision was not what you think —
But oh! it was all.   It was the meaning of life,
Excellent consummation of desires
For ever, let into the heart with pain
Most sweet.   That smile did take the feeding soul
Deeper and deeper into heaven.   The sward
(For I had bowed my face on it) I found
Grew in my spirit's longed for native land —
At last I was at home.'

       And here she paused:
I must needs weep.   I have not been in heaven,
Therefore she could not tell me what she heard,
Therefore she might not tell me what she saw,
Only I understood that One drew near
Who said to her she should e'en come, ' Because,'
Said He, 'My Father loves Me.   I will ask

He send, a guiding Angel for My sake,
Since the dark way is long, and rough, and hard,
So that I shall not lose whom I love — thee.'

Other words wonderful of things not known,
When she had uttered, I gave hope away,
Cried out, and took her in despairing arms,
Asking no more.   Then while the comfortless
Dawn till night fainted grew, alas! a key
That with abhorrèd jarring probed the door.
We kissed, we looked, unlocked our arms.   She sighed
'Remember.'   'Ay, I will remember.   What?'
'To come to me.'   Then I, thrust roughly forth —
I, bereft, dumb, forlorn, unremedied
My hurt for ever, stumbled blindly down,
And the great door was shut behind and chained.

The weird pathetic scarlet of day dawning,
More kin to death of night than birth of morn,
Peered o'er yon hill bristling with spires of pine.
I heard the crying of the men condemned.
Men racked, that should be martyr'd presently,
And my great grief met theirs with might; I held
All our poor earth's despairs in my poor breast.
The choking reek, the faggots were all mine.
Ay, and the partings they were all mine — mine.
Father, it will be very good methinks
To die so, to die soon.   It doth appease

The soul in misery for its fellows, when
There is no help, to suffer even as they.

Father, when I had lost her, when I sat
After my sickness on the pallet bed,
My forehead dropp'd into my hand, behold
Some one beside me.   A man's hand let down
With that same action kind, compassionate,
Upon my shoulder.   And I took the hand
Between mine own, laying my face thereon.
I knew this man for him who spoke with me,
Letting me see my Delia.   I looked up.
Lo! lo! the robed ecclesiastic proud,
He and this other one.   Tell you his name?
Am I a fiend?   No, he was good to me,
Almost he placed his life in my hand.
                                        Father,
He with good pitying words long talked to me,
'Did I not strive to save her?'   'Ay,' quoth I.
'But sith it would not be, I also claim
Death, burning; let me therefore die — let me.
I am wicked, would be heretic, but, faith,
I know not how, and Holy Church I hate.
She is no mother of mine, she slew my love.'
What answer?   'Peace, peace, thou art hard on me.
Favour I forfeit with the Mother of God,
Lose rank among the saints, foresee my soul
Drenched in the unmitigated flame, and take

My payment in the lives snatched at all risk
From battling in it here. O, an thou turn
And tear from me, lost to that other world
My heart's reward in this, I am twice lost;
Now have I doubly failed.'

                      Father, I know
The Church would rail, hound forth, disgrace, try, burn,
Make his proud name, discover'd, infamy,
Tread underfoot his ashes, curse his soul.
But God is greater than the Church. I hope
He shall not, for that he loved men, lose God.
I hope to hear it said 'Thy sins are all
Forgiven; come in, thou hast done well.'

                        For me
My chronicle comes down to its last page.
'Is not life sweet?' quoth he, and comforted
My sick heart with good words, 'duty' and 'home.'
Then took me at moonsetting down the stair
To the dark deserted midway of the street,
Gave me a purse of money, and his hand
Laid on my shoulder, holding me with words
A father might have said, bad me God speed,
So pushed me from him, turned, and he was gone.

There was a Pleiad lost; where is she now?
None knoweth, — O she reigns, it is my creed,
Otherwhere dedicate to making day.
The God of Gods, He doubtless looked to that

Who wasteth never ought He fashionèd.
I have no vision, but where vision fails
Faith cheers, and truly, truly there is need,
The god of this world being so unkind.
O love! My girl for ever to the world
Wanting.   Lost, not that any one should find,
But wasted for the sake of waste, and lost
For love of man's undoing, of man's tears,
By envy of the evil one; I mourn
For thee, my golden girl, I mourn, I mourn.

He set me free.   And it befell anon
That I must imitate him.   Then 't befell
That on the holy Book I read, and all,
The mediating Mother and her Babe,
God and the Church, and man and life and death,
And the dark gulfs of bitter purging flame,
Did take on alteration.   Like a ship
Cast from her moorings, drifting from her port,
Not bound to any land, not sure of land,
My dull'd soul lost her reckoning on that sea
She sailed, and yet the voyage was nigh done.

This God was not the God I had known; this Christ
Was other.   O, a gentler God, a Christ —
By a mother and a Father infinite —
In distance each from each made kin to me.
Blest Sufferer on the rood; but yet, I say

Other.   Far gentler, and I cannot tell,
Father, if you, or she, my golden girl,
Or I, or any aright those mysteries read.

I cannot fathom them.   There is not time,
So quickly men condemned me to this cell.
I quarrell'd not so much with Holy Church
For that she taught, as that my love she burned.
I die because I hid her enemies,
And read the Book.

                        But O, forgiving God,
I do elect to trust thee.   I have thought,
What! are there set between us and the sun
Millions of miles, and did He like a tent
Rear up yon vasty sky?   Is heaven less wide?
And dwells He there, but for His wingèd host,
Almost alone?   Truly I think not so ;
He has had trouble enough with this poor world
To make Him as an earthly father would,
Love it and value it more.

                           He did not give
So much to have us with Him, and yet fail.
And now He knows I would believe e'en so
As pleaseth Him, an there was time to learn
Or certitude of heart ; but time fails, time.
He knoweth also 't were a piteous thing
Not to be sure of my love's welfare — not
To see her happy and good in that new home.

Most piteous.   I could all forego but this.
O let me see her, Lord.

                              What, also I !
White ashes and a waft of vapour — I
To flutter on before the winds.   No, no.
And yet for ever ay — my flesh shall hiss
And I shall hear 't.   Dreadful, unbearable !
Is it to-morrow ?

                         Ay, indeed, indeed,
To-morrow.   But my moods are as great waves
That rise and break and thunder down on me,
And then fall'n back sink low.

                                   I have waked long
And cannot hold my thoughts upon th' event ;
They slip, they wander forth.

                                   How the dusk grows.
This is the last moonrising we shall see.
Methought till morn to pray, and cannot pray.
Where is mine Advocate ? let Him say all
And more was in my mind to say this night,
Because to-morrow —   Ah ! no more of that,
The tale is told.   Father, I fain would sleep,

Truly my soul is silent unto God.

A VINE-ARBOUR IN THE FAR WEST.

I.

'LAURA, my Laura!' 'Yes, mother!' 'I want
you, Laura; come down.'
'What is it, mother — what, dearest? O your loved face
how it pales!
You tremble, alas and alas — you heard bad news from
the town?'
'Only one short half hour to tell it. My poor courage
fails —

II.

Laura.' 'Where 's Ronald? — O anything else but
Ronald!' 'No, no,
Not Ronald, if all beside, my Laura, disaster and tears;
But you, it is yours to send them away, for you they will
go,
One short half hour, and must it decide, it must for the
years.

III.

Laura, you think of your father sometimes?' 'Sometimes!'
'Ah, but how?'
'I think — that we need not think, sweet mother — the
time is not yet,

He is as the wraith of a wraith, and a far off shadow now —
—But if you have heard he is dead?' 'Not that?'
'Then let me forget.'

IV.

'The sun is off the south window, draw back the curtain,
  my child.'
'But tell it, mother.' 'Answer you first what it is that
  you see.'
'The lambs on the mountain slope, and the crevice with
  blue ice piled.'
'Nearer.' — 'But, mother!' 'Nearer!' 'My heifer she's
  lowing to me.'

V.

'Nearer.' 'Nothing, sweet mother, O yes, for one sits in
  the bower.
Black the clusters hang out from the vine about his snow-
  white head,
And the scarlet leaves, where my Ronald leaned.' 'Only
  one half hour —
Laura' — 'O mother, my mother dear, all known though
  nothing said.

VI.

O it breaks my heart, the face dejected that looks not on
  us,
A beautiful face—I remember now, though long I forgot.'

'Ay and I loved it. I love him to-day, and to see him
    thus !
Saying "I go if she bids it, for work her woe — I will not."

VII.

There! weep not, wring not your hands, but think, think
    with your heart and soul.'
' Was he innocent, mother ? If he was, I, sure had been
    told,
' He said so.' ' Ah, but they do.' ' And I hope — and long
    was his dole,
And all for the signing a name (if indeed he signed) for
    gold.'

VIII.

' To find us again, in the far far West, where hid, we were
    free —
But if he was innocent — O my heart, it is riven in two,
If he goes how hard upon him — or stays — how harder
    on me,
For O my Ronald, my Ronald, my dear, — my best what
    of you!'

IX.

' Peace; think, my Laura — I say he will go there, weep
    not so sore.
And the time is come, Ronald knows nothing, your father
    will go,

As the shadow fades from its place will he, and be seen
  no more.'
'There 'll be time to think to-morrow, and after, but to-
  day, no.

x.

I 'm going down the garden, mother.' 'Laura!' 'I 've
  dried my tears.'
'O how will this end!' 'I know not the end, I can but
  begin.'
'But what will you say?' 'Not "welcome, father,"
  though long were those years,
But I 'll say to him, "O my poor father, we wait you,
  come in."

LOVERS AT THE LAKE SIDE.

I.

'AND you brought him home.' 'I did, ay Ronald, it
  rested with me.'
'Love!' 'Yes.' 'I would fain you were not so calm.'
  'I cannot weep. No.'
'What is he like, your poor father?' 'He is — like —
  this fallen tree
Prone at our feet, by the still lake taking on rose from
  the glow,

II.

Now scarlet, O look! overcoming the blue both lake and
sky,
While the waterfalls waver like smoke, then leap in and
are not.
And shining snow-points of high sierras cast down, there
they lie.'
'O Laura — I cannot bear it. Laura! as if I forgot.'

III.

'No, you remember, and I remember that evening — like
this
When we come forth from the gloomy Canyon, lo, a
sinking sun.
And, Ronald, you gave to me your troth ring, I gave my
troth kiss.'
'Give me another, I say that this makes no difference,
none.

IV.

It hurts me keenly. It hurts to the soul that you thought
it could.'
'I never thought so, my Ronald, my love, never thought
you base.'
No, but I look for a nobler nobleness, loss understood,
Accepted, and not that common truth which can hold
through disgrace.

v.

O! we remember, and how ere that noon through deeps
    of the lake
We floating looked down and the boat's shadow followed
    on rocks below,
So clear the water. O all pathetic as if for love's sake
Our life that is but a fleeting shadow 't would under us
    show.

vi.

O we remember forget-me-not pale, and white columbine
You wreathed for my hair; because we remember this
    cannot be.
Ah! here is your ring — see, I draw it off — it must not
    be mine,
Put it on, love, if but for the moment and listen to me.

vii.

I look for the best, I look for the most, I look for the
    all
From you, it consoles this misery of mine, there is you to
    trust.
O if you can weep, let us weep together, tears may well
    fall
For that lost sunsetting and what it promised, — they
    may, they must.

VIII.

Do you say nothing, mine own belovèd, you know what I
　　mean,
And whom. — To her pride and her love from you shall
　　such blow be dealt . . . .
. . . . Silence uprisen, is like a presence, it comes us
　　between . . .
As once there was darkness, now is there silence that
　　may be felt.

IX.

Ronald, your mother, so gentle, so pure, and you are her
　　best,
'T is she whom I think of, her quiet sweetness, her
　　gracious way.
How could she bear it?' — 'Laura!' 'Yes, Ronald.'
　　'Let that matter rest.
You might give your name to my father's child?' 'My
　　father's name. Ay,

X.

Who died before it was soiled.' 'You mutter.' 'Why,
　　love, are you here?'
'Because my mother fled forth to the West, her trouble
　　to hide,
And I was so small, the lone pine forest, and tier upon
　　tier,
Far off Mexican snowy sierras pushed England aside.'

XI.

'And why am I here?' 'But what did you mutter?'
'O pardon, sweet.

Why came I here and — my mother?' In truth then I
cannot tell.'

'Yet you drew my ring from your finger — see — I kneel
at your feet.'

'Put it on. 'T was for no fault of mine.' 'Love! I
knew that full well.'

XII.

'And yet there be faults that long repented, are aye to
deplore,

Wear my ring, Laura, at least till I choose some words I
can say,

If indeed any word need be said.' 'No! wait, Ronald,
no more;

What! is there respite? Give me a moment to think
"nay" or "ay,"

XIII.

I know not, but feel there is. O pardon me, pardon me, —
peace.

For nought is to say, and the dawn of hope is a solemn
thing,

Let us have silence. Take me back, Ronald, full sweet
  is release.'
' Laura ! but give me my troth kiss again.'   ' And give
  me my ring.'

THE WHITE MOON WASTETH.

THE white moon wasteth,
    And cold morn hasteth
  Athwart the snow,
The red east burneth
And the tide turneth,
    And thou must go.

Think not, sad rover,
Their story all over
  Who come from far —
Once, in the ages
Won goodly wages
  Led by a star.

Once, for all duly
Guidance doth truly
  Shine as of old,
Opens for me and thee
Once, opportunity
  Her gates of gold.

Enter, thy star is out,
Traverse nor faint nor doubt
　　Earth's antres wild,
Thou shalt find good and rest
As found the Magi blest
　　That divine Child.

———◦———

AN ARROW-SLIT.

I CLOMB full high the belfry tower
　　Up to you arrow-slit, up and away,
I said ' let me look on my heart's fair flower
　　In the walled garden where she doth play.'

My care she knoweth not, no nor the cause,
　　White rose, red rose about her hung,
And I aloft with the doves and the daws.
　　They coo and call to their callow young.

Sing, ' O an she were a white rosebud fair
　　Dropt, and in danger from passing feet,
'T is I would render her service tender,
　　Upraised on my bosom with reverence meet.'

Playing at the ball, my dearest of all,
　　When she grows older how will it be,
I dwell far away from her thoughts to-day
　　That heed not, need not, or mine or me.

Sing, 'O an my love were a fledgeling dove
  That flutters forlorn o' her shallow nest,
'T is I would render her service tender,
  And carry her, carry her on my breast.'

WENDOVER.

UPLIFTED and lone, set apart with our love
  On the crest of a soft swelling down
Cloud shadows that meet on the grass at our feet
  Sail on above Wendover town.

Wendover town takes the smile of the sun
  As if yearning and strife were no more,
From her red roofs float high neither plaint neither sigh,
  All the weight of the world is our own.

Would that life were more kind and that souls might
    have peace
  As the wide mead from storm and from bale,
We bring up our own care, but how sweet over there
  And how strange is their calm in the vale.

As if trouble at noon had achieved a deep sleep,
  Lapped and lulled from the weariful fret,
Or shot down out of day, had a hint dropt away
  As if grief might attain to forget.

Not if we two indeed had gone over the bourne
  And were safe on the hills of the blest,
Not more strange they might show to us drawn from
    below,
  Come up from long dolour to rest.

But the peace of that vale would be thine love and mine,
  And sweeter the air than of yore,
And this life we have led as a dream that is fled
  Might appear to our thought evermore.

' Was it life, was it life?' we might say ''t was scarce life,'
  ' Was it love? 't was scarce love,' looking down,
' Yet we mind a sweet ray of the red sun one day
  Low lying on Wendover town.

———◦◦———

THE LOVER PLEADS.

I.

WHEN I had guineas many a one
      Nought else I lacked 'neath the sun,
I had two eyes the bluest seen,
A perfect shape, a gracious mien,
I had a voice might charm the bale
From a two days widowed nightingale,
And if you ask how this I know
I had a love who told me so.

The lover pleads. the maid hearkeneth,
Her foot turns, his day darkeneth.
Love unkind, O can it be
'T was your foot false did turn from me.

II.

The gear is gone, the red gold spent,
Favour and beauty with them went,
Eyes take the veil, their shining done,
Not fair to him is fair to none,
Sweet as a bee's bag 't was to taste
His praise. O honey run to waste,
He loved not! spoiled is all my way
In the spoiling of that yesterday.

The shadows wax, the low light alters,
Gold west fades, and false heart falters.
The pity of it! — Love 's a rover,
The last word said, and all over.

SONG IN THREE PARTS.

I.

THE white broom flatt'ring her flowers in calm June
    weather,
          ' O most sweet wear;
Forty-eight weeks of my life do none desire me,
          Four am I fair.'

          Quoth the brown bee
          ' In thy white wear
          Four thou art fair.
          A mystery
          Of honeyed snow
          In scented air
          The bee lines flow
          Straight unto thee.
          Great boon and bliss
          All pure I wis,
          And sweet to grow
          Ay, so to give
          That many live.
          Now as for me,
          I,' quoth the bee,
          ' Have not to give,

Through long hours sunny
Gathering I live :
Aye debonair
Sailing sweet air
After my fare,
Bee-bread and honey.
In thy deep coombe,
O thou white broom,
Where no leaves shake,
Brake,
Bent nor clover,
I a glad rover,
Thy calms partake,
While winds of might
From height to height
Go bodily over.
Till slanteth light,
And up the rise
Thy shadow lies,
A shadow of white,
A beauty-lender
Pathetic, tender.

Short is thy day ?
Answer with ' Nay,'
Longer the hours
That wear thy flowers
Than all dull, cold

Years manifold
That gift withhold.
A long liver,
O honey-giver,
Thou by all showing
Art made, bestowing,
I envy not
Thy greater lot,
Nor thy white wear.
But, as for me,
I,' quoth the bee,
' Never am fair.'

II.

The nightingale lorn of his note in darkness brooding
     Deeply and long,
' Two sweet months spake the heart to the heart.   Alas!
   all 's over,
     O lost my song.'

One in the tree,
' Hush now!   Let be:
The song at ending
Left my long tending
Over also.
Let be, let us go
Across the wan sea.

The little ones care not,
And I fare not
Amiss with thee.

Thou hast sung all,
This hast thou had.
Love, be not sad ;
It shall befall
Assuredly,
When the bush buddeth
And the bank studdeth —
Where grass is sweet
And damps do fleet,
Her delicate beds
With daisy heads
That the Stars Seven
Leaned down from heaven
Shall sparkling mark
In the warm dark
Thy most dear strain
Which ringeth aye true —
Piercing vale, croft
Lifted aloft
Dropt even as dew
With a sweet quest
To her on the nest
When damps we love
Fall from above.

" Art thou asleep ?
Answer me, answer me,
Night is so deep
Thy right fair form
I cannot see ;
Answer me, answer me,
Are the eggs warm ?
Is 't well with thee ? "

Ay, this shall be
Assuredly.
Ay, thou full fain
In the soft rain
Shalt sing again.'

III.

A fair wife making her moan, despised, forsaken,
    Her good days o'er ;
' Seven sweet years of my life did I live belovèd,
    Seven — no more.'

Then Echo woke — and spoke
    ' No more — no more,'
And a wave broke
    On the sad shore
When Echo said
    ' No more.'

Nought else made reply,
Nor land, nor loch, nor sky
Did any comfort try,
But the wave spread
Echo's faint tone
Alone,
All down the desolate shore,
' No more — no more.'

———◦◦◦———

'IF I FORGET THEE, O JERUSALEM.'

OUT of the melancholy that is made
    Of ebbing sorrow that too slowly ebbs,
Comes back a sighing whisper of the reed,
A note in new love-pipings on the bough,
Grieving with grief till all the full-fed air
And shaken milky corn doth wot of it,
The pity of it trembling in the talk
Of the beforetime merrymaking brook —
Out of that melancholy will the soul,
In proof that life is not forsaken quite
Of the old trick and glamour which made glad;
Be cheated some good day and not perceive
How sorrow ebbing out is gone from view,
How tired trouble fall'n for once on sleep,
How keen self-mockery that youth's eager dream

Interpreted to mean so much is found
To mean and give so little — frets no more,
Floating apart as on a cloud — O then
Not e'en so much as murmuring ' Let this end,'
She will, no longer weighted, find escape,
Lift up herself as if on wings and flit
Back to the morning time.

　　　　　　　　　'O once with me
It was all one, such joy I had at heart,
As I heard sing the morning star, or God
Did hold me with an Everlasting Hand,
And dip me in the day.

　　　　　　　　O once with me,'
Reflecting ' 't was enough to live, to look
Wonder and love.   Now let that come again.
Rise ! '   And ariseth first a tanglement
Of flowering bushes, peonies pale that drop
Upon a mossy lawn, rich iris spikes,
Bee-borage, mealy-stemmed auricula,
Brown wallflower, and the sweetbriar ever sweet,
Her pink buds pouting from their green.

　　　　　　　　　　　To these
Add thick espaliers where the bullfinch came
To strew much budding wealth, and was not chid.
Then add wide pear trees on the warmèd wall,
The old red wall one cannot see beyond.
That is the garden.

　　　　　　　In the wall a door

Green, blistered with the sun. You open it,
And lo ! a sunny waste of tumbled hills
And a glad silence, and an open calm.
Infinite leisure, and a slope where rills
Dance down delightedly, in every crease,
And lambs stoop drinking and the finches dip.
Then shining waves upon a lonely beach.
That is the world.

     An all-sufficient world,
And as it seems an undiscovered world,
So very few the folk that come to look.
Yet one has heard of towns ; but they are far
The world is undiscovered, and the child
Is undiscovered that with stealthy joy
Goes gathering like a bee who in dark cells
Hideth sweet food to live on in the cold.
What matters to the child, it matters not
More than it mattered to the moons of Mars,
That they for ages undiscovered went
Marked not of man, attendant on their king.

A shallow line of sand curved to the cliff,
There dwelt the fisherfolk, and there inland
Some scattered cottagers in thrift and calm,
Their talk full oft was of old days, — for here
Was once a fosse, and by this rock-hewn path
Our wild fore-elders as 't is said would come
To gather jetsam from some Viking wreck,

Like a sea-beast wide breasted (her snake head
Reared up as staring while she rocked ashore)
That split, and all her ribs were on their fires
The red whereof at their wives' throats made bright
Gold gauds which from the weed they picked ere yet
The tide had turned.

        'Many,' methought, 'and rich
They must have been, so long their chronicle.
Perhaps the world was fuller then of folk,
For ships at sea are few that near us now.'

Yet sometimes when the clouds were torn to rags,
Flying black before a gale, we saw one rock
In the offing, and the mariner folk would cry,
'Look how she labours; those aboard may hear
Her timbers creak e'en as she 'd break her heart.'

'T was then the grey gulls blown ashore would light
In flocks, and pace the lawn with flat cold feet.

And so the world was sweet, and it was strange,
Sweet as a bee-kiss to the crocus flower,
Surprising, fresh, direct, but ever one.
The laughter of glad music did not yet
In its echo yearn, as hinting ought beyond,
Nor pathos tremble at the edge of bliss
Like a moon halo in a watery sky,
Nor the sweet pain alike of love and fear

In a world not comprehended touch the heart —
The poetry of life was not yet born.
'T was a thing hidden yet that there be days
When some are known to feel ' God is about,'
As if that morn more than another morn
Virtue flowed forth from Him, the rolling world
Swam in a soothèd calm made resonant
And vital, swam as in the lap of God
Come down ; until she slept and had a dream
(Because it was too much to bear awake).
That all the air shook with the might of Him
And whispered how she was the favourite world
That day, and bade her drink His essence in.

'Tis on such days that seers prophesy
And poets sing, and many who are wise
Find out for man's wellbeing hidden things
Whereof the hint came in that Presence known
Yet unknown. But a seer — what is he ?
A poet is a name of long ago.

Men love the largeness of the field — the wild
Quiet that soothes the moor. In other days
They loved the shadow of the city wall,
In its stone ramparts read their poetry,
Safety and state, gold, and the arts of peace,
Law-giving, leisure, knowledge, all were there

This to excuse a child's allegiance and
A spirit's recurrence to the older way.
Orphan'd, with aged guardians kind and true,
Things came to pass not told before to me.

Thus, we did journey once when eve was near.
Through carriage windows I beheld the moors,
Then, churches, hamlets cresting of low hills.
The way was long, at last I, fall'n asleep,
Awoke to hear a rattling 'neath the wheels
And see the lamps alight.   This was the town.

Then a wide inn received us, and full soon
Came supper, kisses, bed.
                          The lamp without
Shone in ; the door was shut, and I alone.
An ecstasy of exultation took
My soul, for there were voices heard and steps,
I was among so many, — none of them
Knew I was come !
                          I rose, with small bare feet,
Across the carpet stole, a white-robed child,
And through the window peered.   Behold the town.

There had been rain, the pavement glistened yet
In a soft lamplight down the narrow street ;
The church was nigh at hand, a clear-toned clock
Chimed slowly, open shops across the way

Showed store of fruit, and store of bread, — and one
Many caged birds.   About were customers,
I saw them bargain, and a rich high voice
Was heard, — a woman sang, her little babe
Slept 'neath her shawl, and by her side a boy
Added wild notes and sweet to hers.

                             Some passed
Who gave her money.   It was far from me
To pity her, she was a part of that
Admired town.   E'en so within the shop
A rosy girl, it may be ten years old,
Quaint, grave.   She helped her mother, deftly weighed
The purple plums, black mulberries rich and ripe
For boyish customers, and counted pence
And dropped them in an apron that she wore.
Methought a queen had ne'er so grand a lot,
She knew it, she looked up at me, and smiled.

But yet the song went on, and in a while
The meaning came ; the town was not enough
To satisfy that singer, for a sigh
With her wild music came.   What wanted she ?
Whate'er she wanted wanted all.   O how
'T was poignant, her rich voice ; not like a bird's.
Could she not dwell content and let them be,
That they might take their pleasure in the town,
For — no, she was not poor, witness the pence.

I saw her boy and that small saleswoman;
He wary, she with grave persuasive air,
Till he came forth with filberts in his cap,
And joined his mother, happy, triumphing.

This was the town; and if you ask what else,
I say good sooth that it was poetry
Because it was the all, and something more, —
It was the life of man, it was the world
That made addition to the watching heart,
First conscious its own beating, first aware
How, beating it kept time with all the race;
Nay, 't was a consciousness far down and dim
Of a Great Father watching too.

But lo! the rich lamenting voice again;
She sang not for herself; it was a song
For me, for I had seen the town and knew,
Yearning I knew the town was not enough.

What more?   To-day looks back on yesterday,
Life's yesterday, the waiting time, the dawn,
And reads a meaning into it, unknown
When it was with us.
                                    It is always so.
But when as ofttimes I remember me
Of the warm wind that moved the beggar's hair,
Of the wet pavement, and the lamps alit,

I know it was not pity that made yearn
My heart for her, and that same dimpled boy
How grand methought to be abroad so late,
And barefoot dabble in the shining wet;
How fine to peer as other urchins did
At those pent huddled doves they let not rest;
No, it was almost envy. Ay, how sweet
The clash of bells; they rang to boast that far
That cheerful street was from the cold sea-fog,
From dark ploughed field and narrow lonesome lane.
How sweet to hear the hum of voices kind,
To see the coach come up with din of horn,
Quick tramp of horses, mark the passers-by
Greet one another, and go on.
                              But now
They closed the shops, the wild clear voice was still,
The beggars moved away — where was their home.
The coach which came from out dull darksome fells
Into the light; passed to the dark again
Like some old comet which knows well her way,
Whirled to the sun that as her fateful loop
She turns, forebodes the destined silences.
Yes, it was gone; the clattering coach was gone,
And those it bore I pitied even to tears,
Because they must go forth, nor see the lights,
Nor hear the chiming bells.
                              In after days,
Remembering of the childish envy and

The childish pity, it has cheered my heart
To think e'en now pity and envy both
It may be are misplaced, or needed not.
Heaven may look down in pity on some soul
Half envied, or some wholly pitied smile,
For that it hath to wait as it were an hour
To see the lights that go not out by night,
To walk the golden street and hear a song;
Other-world poetry that is the all
And something more.

NATURE, FOR NATURE'S SAKE.

WHITE as white butterflies that each one dons
    Her face their wide white wings to shade withal,
Many moon-daisies throng the water-spring,
    While couched in rising barley titlarks call,
And bees alit upon their martagons
    Do hang a-murmuring, a-murmuring.

They chide, it may be, alien tribes that flew
    And rifled their best blossom, counted on
And dreamed on in the hive ere dangerous dew
    That clogs bee-wings had dried ; but when outshone
Long shafts of gold (made all for them) of power
To charm it away, those thieves had suckèd the flower.

Now must they go ; a-murmuring they go,
   And little thrushes twitter in the nest ;
The world is made for them, and even so
   The clouds are ; they have seen no stars, the breast
Of their soft mother hid them all the night,
Till her mate came to her in red dawn-light.

Eggs scribbled over with strange writing, signs,
   Prophecies, and their meaning (for you see
The yolk within) is life, 'neath yonder bines
   Lie among sedges ; on a hawthorn tree
The slender lord and master perched hard by,
Scolds at all comers if they step too nigh.

And our small river makes encompassment
   Of half the mead and holm : yon lime-trees grow
All heeling over to it, diligent
   To cast green doubles of themselves below,
But shafts of sunshine reach its shallow floor
And warm the yellow sand it ripples o'er.

Ripples and ripples to a pool it made
   Turning. The cows are there, one creamy white —
She should be painted with no touch of shade
   If any list to limn her — she the light
Above, about her, treads out circles wide,
And sparkling water flashes from her side.

The clouds have all retired to so great height
  As earth could have no dealing with them more,
As they were lost, for all her drawing and might,
  And must be left behind; but down the shore
Lie lovelier clouds in ranks of lace-work frail,
Wild parsley with a myriad florets pale,

Another milky-way, more intricate
  And multitudinous, with every star
Perfect. Long changeful sunbeams undulate
  Amid the stems where sparklike creatures are
That hover and hum for gladness, then the last
Tree rears her graceful head, the shade is passed.

And idle fish in warm wellbeing lie
  Each with his shadow under, while at ease
As clouds that keep their shape the darting fry
  Turn and are gone in company; o'er these
Strangers to them, strangers to us, from holes
Scooped in the bank peer out shy water-voles.

Here, take for life and fly with innocent feet
  The brown-eyed fawns, from moving shadows clear;
There, down the lane with multitudinous bleat
  Plaining on shepherd lads a flock draws near;
A mild lamenting fills the morning air,
'Why to you upland fold must we needs fare?'

These might be fabulous creatures every one,
  And this their world might be some other sphere
We had but heard of, for all said or done
  To know of them, — of what this many a year
They may have thought of man, or of his sway,
Or even if they have a God and pray,

The sweetest river bank can never more
  Home to its source tempt back the lapsèd stream,
Nor memory reach the ante-natal shore,
  Nor one awake behold a sleeper's dream,
Not easier 't were that unbridged chasm to walk,
And share the strange lore of their wordless talk.

Like to a poet voice, remote from ken,
  That unregarded sings and undesired,
Like to a star unnamed by lips of men,
  That faints at dawn in saffron light retired,
Like to an echo in some desert deep
From age to age unwakened from its sleep —

So falls unmarked that other world's great song,
  And lapsing wastes without interpreter.
Slave world! not man's to raise, yet man's to wrong,
  He cannot to a loftier place prefer,
But he can, — all its earlier rights forgot,
Reign reckless if its nations rue their lot.

If they can sin or feel life's wear and fret,
 An men had loved them better, it may be
We had discovered. But who e'er did yet,
 After the sage saints in their clemency,
Ponder in hope they had a heaven to win,
Or make a prayer with a dove's name therein.

As grave Augustine pleading in his day,
 ' Have pity, Lord, upon the unfledged bird,
Lest such as pass do trample it in the way,
 Not marking, or not minding; give the word,
O bid an angel in the nest again
To place it, lest the mother's love be vain.

And let it live, Lord God, till it can fly.'
 This man dwelt yearning, fain to guess, to spell
The parable; all work of God Most High
 Took to his man's heart. Surely this was well;
To love is more than to be loved, by leave
Of Heaven, to give is more than to receive.

He made it so that said it. As for us
 Strange is their case toward us, for they give
And we receive. Made martyrs ever thus
 In deed but not in will, for us they live,
For us they die, we quench their little day,
Remaining blameless, and they pass away.

The world is better served than it is ruled,
 And not alone of them, for ever
Ruleth the man, the woman serveth fooled
 Full oft of love, not knowing his yoke is sore.
Life's greatest Son nought from life's measure swerved,
He was among us 'as a man that served.'

Have they another life, and was it won
 In the sore travail of another death,
Which loosed the manacles from our race undone
 And plucked the pang from dying?   If this breath
Be not their all, reproach no more debarred,
'O unkind lords, you made our bondage hard'

May be their plaint when we shall meet again
 And make our peace with them; the sea of life
Find flowing, full, nor ought or lost or vain.
 Shall the vague hint whereof all thought is rife,
The sweet pathetic guess indeed come true,
And things restored reach that great residue?

Shall we behold fair flights of phantom doves,
 Shall furred creatures couch in moly flowers.
Swan souls the rivers oar with their world-loves,
 In difference welcome as these souls of ours?
Yet soul of man from soul of man far more
May differ, even as thought did heretofore

That ranged and varied on th' undying gleam:
    From a pure breath of God aspiring, high,
Serving and reigning, to the tender dream,
    The wingèd Psyche and her butterfly —
From thrones and powers, to — fresh from death alarms
Child spirits entering in an angel's arms.

Why must we think, begun in paradise,
    That their long line, cut off with severance fell,
Shall end in nothingness — the sacrifice
    Of their long service in a passing knell?
Could man be wholly blest if not to say
'Forgive' — nor make amends for ever and aye?

Waste, waste on earth, and waste of God afar.
    Celestial flotsam, blazing spars on high,
Drifts in the meteor month from some wrecked star,
    Strew oft th' unwrinkled ocean of the sky,
And pass no more accounted of than be
Long dulses limp that stripe a mundane sea.

The sun his kingdom fills with light, but all
    Save where it strikes some planet and her moons
Across cold chartless gulfs ordained to fall,
    Void antres, reckoneth no man's nights or noons,
But feeling forth as for some outmost shore,
Faints in the blank of doom, and is no more.

God scattereth His abundance as forgot,
  And what then doth he gather? If we know,
'T is that One told us it was life. 'For not
  A sparrow,' quoth he, uttering long ago
The strangest words that e'er took earthly sound,
'Without your Father falleth to the ground.'

PERDITA.

I GO beyond the commandment.' So be it. Then mine
    be the blame,
The loss, the lack, the yearning, till life's last sand be
    run, —
I go beyond the commandment, yet honour stands fast with
    her claim,
And what I have rued I shall rue ; for what I have done
    — I have done.

Hush, hush ! for what of the future ; you cannot the base
    exalt,
There is no bridging a chasm over, that yawns with so
    sheer incline ;
I will not any sweet daughter's cheek should pale for this
    mother's fault,
Nor son take leave to lower his life a-thinking on mine.

' *Will I tell you all?* ' So! this, e'en this, will I do for
    your great love's sake;
Think what it costs. ' *Then let there be silence — silence*
    you 'll count consent.'
No, and no, and for ever no: rather to cross and to
    break,
And to lower your passion I speak — that other it was I
    meant.

That other I meant (but I know not how) to speak of,
    nor April days,
Nor a man's sweet voice that pleaded — O (but I prom-
    ised this) —
He never talked of marriage, never; I grant him that
    praise;
And he bent his stately head, and I lost, and he won with
    a kiss.

He led me away — O, how poignant sweet the nightin-
    gale's note that noon —
I beheld, and each crispèd spire of grass to him for my
    sake was fair,
And warm winds flattered my soul blowing straight from
    the soul of June,
And a lovely lie was spread on the fields, but the blue
    was bare.

When I looked up, he said: 'Love, fair love! O rather
    look in these eyes
With thine far sweeter than eyes of Eve when she stepped
    the valley unshod' —
For ONE might be looking through it, he thought, and he
    would not in any wise
I should mark it open, limitless, empty, bare 'neath the
    gaze of God.

Ah me! I was happy — yes, I was; 't is fit you should
    know it all,
While love was warm and tender and yearning. the rough
    winds troubled me not ;
I heard them moan without in the forest ; heard the chill
    rains fall —
But I thought my place was sheltered with him — I
    forgot, I forgot.

After came news of a wife ; I think he was glad I should
    know,
To stay my pleading, 'take me to church and give me
    my ring' ;
'You should have spoken before,' he had sighed. when I
    prayed him so,
For his heart was sick for himself and me, and this bitter
    thing.

But my dream was over me still, — I was half beguiled,
And he in his kindness left me seldom, O seldom, alone,
And yet love waxed cold, and I saw the face of my little
　　child,
And then at the last I knew what I was, and what I had
　　done.

'You *will give me the name of wife*. You *will give me a
　　ring.*' — O peace!
You are not let to ruin your life because I ruined mine;
You will go to your people at home. There will be rest
　　and release;
The bitter now will be sweet full soon — ay, and denial
　　divine.

But spare me the ending. I did not wait to be quite
　　cast away;
I left him asleep, and the bare sun rising shone red on
　　my gown.
There was dust in the lane, I remember; prints of feet in
　　it lay,
And honeysuckle trailed in the path that led on to the
　　down.

I was going nowhere — I wandered up, then turned and
　　dared to look back,
Where low in the valley he careless and quiet — quiet
　　and careless slept.

'*Did I love him yet?*' I loved him. Ay, my heart on
   the upland track
Cried to him, sighed to him out by the wheat, as I
   walked, and I wept.

I knew of another alas, one that had been in my place,
Her little ones, she forsaken, were almost in need ;
I went to her, and carried my babe, then all in my satins
   and lace
I sank at the step of her desolate door, a mourner indeed.

I cried, ' 'T is the way of the world, would I had never
   been born.' '
'Ay, 't is the way of the world, but have you no sense
   to see
For all the way of the world,' she answers and laughs me
   to scorn,
' The world is made the world that it is by fools like you,
   like me.'

Right hard upon me, hard on herself, and cold as the
   cold stone,
But she took me in ; and while I lay sick I knew I was
   lost,
Lost with the man I loved, or lost without him, making
   my moan
Blighted and rent of the bitter frost, wrecked, tempest
   tossed, lost, lost !

How am I fallen : — we that might make of the world
what we would,
Some of us sink in deep waters. Ah ! *'you would raise
me again ? '*
No true heart, — you cannot, you cannot, and all in my
soul that is good
Cries out against such a wrong. Let be, your quest is
for ever in vain.

For I feel with another heart, I think with another mind,
I have worsened life, I have wronged the world, I have
lowered the light ;
But as for him, his words and his ways were after his kind,
He did but spoil where he could, and waste where he
might.

For he was let to do it ; I let him and left his soul
To walk mid the ruins he made of home in remembrance
of love's despairs,
Despairs that harden the hearts of men and shadow their
heads with dole,
And woman's fault, though never on earth, may be
healed, — but what of theirs.

'T was fit you should hear it all — What, tears ? they comfort me ; now you will go,
Nor wrong your life for the nought you call ' a pair of
beautiful eyes,'

'*I will not say I love you.*' Truly I will not, no.

'*Will, I pity you?*' Ay, but the pang will be short, you
shall wake and be wise.

'*Shall we meet?* We shall meet on the other side, but
not before.

I shall be pure and fair, I shall hear the sound of THE
NAME,

And see the form of His face. You too will walk on that
shore,

In the garden of the Lord God, where neither is sorrow
nor shame.

Farewell, I shall bide alone, for God took my one white
lamb,

I work for such as she was, and I will the while I last.

But there's no beginning again, ever I am what I am,

And nothing, nothing, nothing, can do away with the
past.

University Press: John Wilson & Son, Cambridge

www.ingramcontent.com/pod-product-compliance
Lightning Source LLC
Chambersburg PA
CBHW020113030726
47498CB00006B/2086